Bruno of Hollywood

Also by Paul Mantee
Published by Ballantine Books
IN SEARCH OF THE PERFECT RAVIOLI

BRUNO *of* HOLLYWOOD

Paul Mantee

BALLANTINE BOOKS / NEW YORK

Library of Congress Cataloging-in-Publication Data
Mantee, Paul.
    Bruno of Hollywood / Paul Mantee.
        p.   cm.
    ISBN 0-345-38379-6
    1. Motion picture industry—California—Los Angeles—
Fiction.   2. Actors—California—Los Angeles—Fiction.
3. Hollywood (Los Angeles, Calif.)—Fiction.   I. Title.
PS3563.A574B78   1994
813'.54—dc20   93-40834
                                                          CIP

Text design by Mary A. Wirth

Manufactured in the United States of America
First Edition: April 1994
10 9 8 7 6 5 4 3 2 1

"All you need to start an asylum is an empty room and the right kind of people."

My Man Godfrey
UNIVERSAL PICTURES, 1936

Bruno of Hollywood

i
· · ·

"**Y**ou haven't changed a bit," she said in dead earnest. Her eyebrows were cleanly plucked, and in their place were two thinly penciled crescents, moon slices of a time gone by and never to return. And tarnished eyes that moved herky-jerky like classic windup toys, nostalgic and weary, from my face to her bourbon and seven and back again.

You haven't changed a bit. Without a hint of irony.

Cut to the irony, I thought, lest the evening drop off the face of the earth before my ice cubes melt.

"Shit, I mean it—excuse my French," continued Margie. "I mean we all age, but . . . really . . . it's incredible. *You* haven't changed."

"I have."

"You haven't."

Our first tiff in a quarter of a century.

"Inside," I replied, indicating my breastbone and dodging the issue.

Thank Christ we weren't picnicking on a treeless meadow in Griffith Park at high noon. And by all means send a drink to the artist who created the barroom dinge that obscured my four-millimeter hair transplants. By and large, hair replacement is best viewed in total darkness.

"Sure you're not hungry?" I asked, repeating the same question I'd put to her not thirty seconds earlier. I felt our time together would whip along nicely if we shared an activity.

Ports is a middle bar. Downtown of Dan Tana's, uptown of real-deal. A brittle dungeonette of an in-the-biz hangabout for the chic and/or broke: Black Russians, Gallo white, and pretty mouths all in a row. An oasis for those of us either in the asylum or knocking on the door, where we can visit after dark and tell old fibs to new acquaintances and nobody gets skewered, except ever so briefly at the front door.

Men scan. Women peek over the sparkle of long-stemmed glasses—a flick of curiosity toward fresh talent, less time than it takes a frozen daiquiri to jump a straw: is she hot, is he hot, might they be Somebody? De rigueur, addictive, and we wouldn't have it any other way.

Ladies and gentlemen of The Biz, may I present Margie Cosgrove, nonpro, forty-three, lately of Fresno—and prone to tell the truth, I suspect. The eyes are sad, but there was a time. I like the flecks of gray, the short no-nonsense do, although a little nonsense never hurts. And yes, the mouth is taut. But my guess is that Margie received her last flower, a five-dollar orchid as I recall, at the 1953 Granville Jaycee Sadie Hawkins Day Dance, where she was unanimously crowned Miss Daisy Mae, the first brunette ever in the annals.

"What're you tryin' to do, make me fatter'n I am?" asked Daisy Mae. The little burst of laughter was throaty now and boozy, and shortened her by half. The ghost of a giggle that only yesterday thrilled me to the brink of acne. But certainly not fat. Loose maybe, in her little black pants suit. I wouldn't say fat.

Send in the conversation.

"Margie Cosgrove!" Because I didn't have a clue.

"Bruno Sangenito!" Nor did she.

I unzipped my stylish but rough-hewn bag from Manhattan's Roberta di Camarino. Enjoyed its feel. Extracted my Shermans, located my Dunhill among essentials. Binaca in case. Half a joint in case. *Michelle* (555-3329) in case. Rezipped, lit up, killed thirty seconds off the clock, and noticed her shoulders were concave from years of what's the use.

I squinted through secondhand smoke.

A foggy Tuesday at the Granville Tennis and Riding Club, practically deserted après—the score was love-love—or never would you have sashayed into the men's shower room in a towel far too small for your own good. As was I—God, we took forever to make the rules. Would I please pretty please dry that one son of a gun of a spot between your shoulders? Sweet shoulders, sloped from the burden of worshipful eyes. I dried and dried the

slow dry, if you recall. No trouble at all, said I, sensing, creat-
ing, nurturing a big bunch of trouble that bit me like a breath
of forbidden wind as you displayed the most luxurious double-
dimpled ass in St. Timothy's Parish and made me promise three
times not to look.

"Do you still play?"

"Huh?"

"Tennis."

And were you hip, that my slip of a towel betrayed me also?
That it fell from my waist in a huff, and hung for one comical
second before it dropped to the floor. And we were back to front,
you and me, vis-à-vis, and had I but trickled a sigh, I'd have
launched a Missa Cantata or at least a lob volley your way, in-
stead of becoming a nut case for the rest of the semester?

"Hell no."

"Too bad."

"I bowl."

Hot in Fresno, we agreed. Cool in L.A., though heat
waves come and go.

"Margie Cosgrove."

"Johnny *Bruno*," she emphasized, updating.

"How's your drink?"

"Fine."

Four grandchildren was a bunch, we concurred, for
her age, let alone a club of hubbies.

"And six kids," she added. "Harvey's my first—he's a
doll-baby. He was born the day I was supposed to gradu-
ate." She momentarily lost her cigarette. "Not the most
pleasant day of my life." Margie swiped at residual ash.

"About a year after you and I split up. What the hell, I had a kid . . ."

Better him.

". . . no big deal." She took a hit of her bourbon and seven. "Hey, I did a lot of things I don't wanna sit around and brag about."

I took interest in the corners of my cocktail napkin. One Mississippi, two Mississippi . . .

"You don't see many of those in the San Joaquin Valley," Margie observed.

"What?" I asked, knowing, yet prolonging the disparity, for the smoke had cleared.

"Men with purses."

"Ahhhh." I saw fit to apologize. "It was a gift."

"I think it's cute."

"Imagine how I'd look with all this crap stuffed in my pocket," I further explained.

"Can I see it?"

"Sure." I handed the bag across the table, and saw fit to call attention to myself. "Show me a man with a purse, and I'll show you a man who looks good in his jeans."

Margie Cosgrove held it and smelled it. "And pretty goddamn hot in a towel if I remember correctly."

"Don't move," I said, as I moved.

Up for a breather.

Over to the bartender—a road company Rock Hudson, enjoying a moment of stardom with a pair of twins in search of an agent. Two more of the same, please—we shared a laugh—and all the quarters in the register.

Across the room with purpose. To lean with both hands, to caress the best jukebox this side of a '48 Plymouth.

A–5.

B–27.

To punch in Bing Crosby and "Stardust." And "Chattanooga Choo-Choo."

M–3.

P–12.

L–26.

Hampton and Brubeck and Shearing. Here's to those blessed unenlightened years, delicate and haywire. Dinner in the diner, nothin' could be finer than to forget for a little while that change is so easy to say.

1939. *I am Buck Jones and my girlfriend's name is Mary. She looks like my mother. I sleep with my gun and hug my pillow. Sometimes we have dinner in bed.*

1942. *I am Richard Blaine, better known as Rick. I have a place, Rick's Place. I have a romantic past and a heroic future because I did the right thing. I drink Scotch, I think, and women are nuts about me.*

Evelyn Sangenito is the best darn bookkeeper Newman's Hardware ever had. So says Charles Newman. They sit around the kitchen table and smoke and have cocktails, and he swears by her ever since my father left. "That's very sweet, Charles," she says, and purses her lips like Shirley Temple and looks at her old-fashioned (Early

Times, heavy on the sugar). Then she blushes and laughs and her dangly earrings jump up and down.

They'll never get married in a million years, even though he's an Aquarius. Charles spends weekends in Santa Rosa with this maiden sister. Fine with me.

My aunt Rose from San Francisco drives a Cadillac and gets married for a living and hates earrings. "Ev," she says, "you can get away with it. Not everybody can wear all that goddamn costume jewelry." She's not too crazy about Charles, either.

1945. *I am Philip Marlowe. Don't mess with me.*

BURT LANCASTER is a savage, and he slipped inside me at the El Rey—at first just for a normal movie visit: *Brute Force*, 1947. But he hung around even as I put my jacket on a different way, and followed me home and practically forced me to broaden my shoulders and toughen my eyes. Enough to scare the living Bogart out of a person. Yet, he took a shine.

So we had dinner together that night and my mom didn't know what to make of us. She liked the fact that I sat up straight for a change and hated the fact that I squinted at my lamb chops. The big guy left after I fell asleep, then dropped in the following day during study hall, and the day after that while I was forcing down a spinach and mayonnaise sandwich—which I can't imagine Mr. Lancaster ever standing still for. So we dumped it.

Over the years he'd leave and come back and vice versa—till a pattern developed. As if he couldn't decide. And when he finally did make up his mind, he made it a point to body-snatch me only when I least needed him. For instance, where the hell was he at the Granville Tennis and Riding Club of a foggy Tuesday?

Some savage.

A light rain fell on an April evening in 1953 as Burt and I whipped the Plymouth onto Baywood Avenue and pulled up sharply in front of the small yellow and white stucco house. We turned off the motor and opened the car door a crack, just enough to operate the interior light so we could check the left corner of our lower lip in the rearview mirror. It wasn't the most mature pimple we'd ever seen, just bulky enough to suggest a speech impediment.

Ev says I'm dramatic because I rearrange my face every Friday night. I call it *Return of the Phantom of the Opera*. She blames it on the stars. I'm a Capricorn. Take *equal* halves of a big fresh lemon, one half in each hand, and scrub vigorously on the fleet of pimples that drifted in for the weekend, dropped anchor and already won the war. (Joe is in the navy, we think.) Then lean against the bathroom sink, stare at myself in the mirror and brace. Since I've put acid on my own face, the plot thickens. (He went to sea when I was five.) Ev tightens her mouth and says, "Scorpio," then finds something to giggle at. Aunt Rose says, "Cheer up, honey. Your father's been at sea since the day you were born." My face gets disappointed at first, then revs up for about ten seconds till it becomes wrathful and vengeful, and grabs me by the rest of me, bounces me off the bathroom walls, drags me through the hall breathing fire, and hurls me onto the bed to claw at my pillow and die before I get the girl. Pisces rising, moon Libra.

Nevertheless.

A cannonball on its way to becoming a basketball bounced back at Burt and me from the rearview mirror of the Plymouth that drizzly evening in April. There was, however, no turning back. Not a chance. Burt wouldn't hear of it. We eased out of the car—*The Killers*—and strode up the cement path. Strode as we had so many times before, missing the cracks. Head up, shoulders square—*Desert Fury*. Jaw set. That heroic glide—*Kiss the Blood Off My Hands*—for which we're famous. Narrowed our eyes, crushed the doorbell with purpose, and Burt hid in the bushes.

I Walk Alone.

Because Beryl Cosgrove was different. Very hot for a mom. Older of course, yet somehow younger. Inviting, yet not. She had real red hair, I'm sure—I can't resist a thickening plot—and the finishing touch of her daughter. How long a leap, I pondered, from black and white sundae with a cherry on top to a very dry martini, as I listened for footsteps I could barely hear.

Would Beryl do it? I wondered. Let's hope.

"Hi, Bruno. My, don't you look handsome!"

I stood adrift in the wetness of the night.

"Come on in!"

She pulled me ashore.

"Margie, Bruno's here!" Beryl called to another darker part of the house which I'd never seen. "Well, sit down, won't you?"

I chose the big chair opposite the sofa.

"We can have a chat."

Would she do it?

"Margie'll be ready in a jiffy. You know how women are."

Show me.

Now why didn't we have glasses at home like the long lean graceful tumbler Beryl Cosgrove placed into my hand? It was amber and fit snugly. Chock full of Par-T-Pak Cola on crackling ice. Not everybody has crackling ice.

Would she do it, or would she fuss around in the kitchen, or answer the dumb phone? She'd done it before, once with black slacks on, which counted, but not nearly as much.

She moved toward the sofa. Fluid Drive. Things were looking up.

Would she flop onto the left cushion? Or the right cushion?

She flopped onto the center cushion.

And did it.

And threw me helter-skelter into a deeper sea, as she lifted a Lucky—picture a stem on an olive in a silver tray—from the case on the coffee table between us, and bound me, gagged me, hung me by the neck with eyes that held secrets to secrets. She tamped her cigarette twice and dead center on a polished fingernail that had touched privacy. Put it to her mouth, lit up with a table lighter that worked on the first click. Exhaled smoke in a slim stream up and away, touched her fingertip to the tip of her tongue to lift a dot of tobacco, which I never did see, crossed those long delicate legs one over the other, and shared with me for a split second her most personal freckles. Those that lie in wait inside darkness, where nylons fear to tread and garter belt dares to begin. Then languished her arm out and across a sculptured knee, Lucky perched à la mode.

Obviously unaware.

"How's your mom?" she asked.

Which I resented.

"Fine."

And that was only the half of it.

I dove into my Par-T-Pak Cola, needing a drink, praying I wouldn't slurp, when out of a sudden puff of pink angora Our Lady of the Possible appeared to the faithful.

Margie Cosgrove had no truck with arrivals. She simply

materialized. No flush, no bang, no click-clack. The carpet was barely aware.

Hair brown as a manzanita sunrise. Shades of light, shades of darkness, one never knew. Mouth a brazen lollipop. Incipient glamour set to the strings of shimmering innocence. Body slender, body full. Familiar, surprising. A galaxy of yeses and nos.

"Hi, there," she giggled.

Naturally, what wit I had vanished.

Should I put my Par-T-Pak Cola down first, and then stand up, I asked myself, as easy answers skidded toward the philosophical, or should I stand up first, and then put my Par-T-Pak Cola down? In which case, I'd have to bend down to get rid of the glass. No good. How about standing up with my long lean tumbler in hand? Then changing hands as the situation dictated? Why not? Too complicated. Okay. How about taking it out the front door and dumping the whole goddamn thing on the lawn when nobody's looking and denying it later?

I stuck it on the floor in self-hatred, spilling very little. I winced, unwound, and floundered to attention, then bent at the waist, sacrificing excellent posture for a hidden lump of confusion.

Margie smelled of Wood Hue, a cologne of the times.

I heard *Would You*.

"Hi," I answered, also giggling, if memory serves. And not quite looking at my shoes, as the wiser, naughtier half of the duo scurried into the kitchen for a sponge, skirt flailing, and youth smiled up at me with chocolate candy eyes, while my better half cowered in the shrubbery.

. . . *CHATTANOOGA Choo-Choo, won't you choo-choo me home. Chattanoogaaaaa . . .*

"Our kind of music," I mused.

"Yeah, I hate that rock crap. My kids love that shit. I can't understand the words half the time."

"So . . . hey, Margie, what about that Jimmy Carter," I said enthusiastically, stupidly, as if we'd worked on the phone bank together. "Speaking of change, I mean." Trying to choo-choo myself uphill, up tempo, into present surroundings.

"I think they're all a bunch of assholes. They sure pour a short drink in this place."

"So you're a bowler," I stated, at a loss for words, a loss for time.

"Yeah."

FADE IN: Bowling shirt.

"Uptown Motors, where I work."

CAMERA REVEALS: Uptown Motors logo.

What does one say to a bowler?

"What's your average?"

"A hundred twenty-five."

"Good." I think.

MAIN TITLE: *Our Lady of the Lanes.*

"We're second in league play."

If all we have in common is Glenn Miller and the Casa Loma what's-its ...

One creates a yawn by recalling one. One nudges it to completion by conjuring up a cliché (they sure don't make movies like they used to) and allowing the scene to play itself. One stifles a yawn at some risk. "Terrific," I lied through lockjaw, and leaned on the table and cupped my face and squeezed it into ten miles of bad road till my ears popped.

"We oughta go," she said.

Works every time.

"Probably," I agreed. "It's late."

"No, I mean bowling. Sometime."

It's late.

"Besides, it's early."

Late.

"Only eight."

CUT TO:

Exhaustion.

DISSOLVE TO:

Eight A.M. Department of Employment Fanfold Form 4581, Rev. #30

Did you work last week?
How much did you earn last week?
Was there any reason you could not have worked that week?

Did you try to find work that week?

Did any person in this office or anywhere else offer you a referral to a job that week?

CLOSE-UP:

Understanding older gentleman at Window P.

Margie spiked her swizzle stick, removed it from her melting ice cubes and sucked it. "My kids don't believe me when I tell them I know a movie star."

"It's a very important moment—a new chapter. In fact, for me, it's the first chapter. For what has my life been up to now? A preface?"

Ball of Fire
RKO RADIO PICTURES, 1941

ii

• • •

Lana Turner is dating Johnny Stompanato. Elizabeth Taylor and Mike Todd have a beautiful baby girl. Elvis Presley says nuts to going steady. And rock 'n' roll is here to stay. So says Hedda Hopper. I read in the newspaper that there are more TV shows made these days than actual movies. I saw myself large on *Dragnet. Gunsmoke.* What fun it would be, I thought, to jump on the streetcar—the Red Car, they call it here—and take it as far as it goes and back again. *This Is Your Life.*

A great door opened.

"D I D F A T H E R Tivinen tell you I was a nudist as well as a cocksucker?" Jay asked, lounging in the doorway of his elegant Hollywood Hills home, wearing a shaved head and half an erection.

Well, of course he hadn't. All Father Tiv said was that

Jay Semple was probably the most famous parishoner ever to take Communion at St. Timothy's, next to Beans Marsachino, who played a season with the Phillies, and he'd probably be thrilled spitless to get me started in movies.

I'd never seen a shaved head before, except on Yul Brynner in *The King and I,* and I couldn't take my eyes off Jay's. Wouldn't dare is more to the point, since he'd apparently decided he liked the cut of my jib while I was still circling the block, rehearsing hello. Now he leaned, relishing the smallness of Granville, California, which I wore so well, and sipped herb tea out of a miniature Grecian urn long before the fashion came. He swung to and fro in no breeze. Everything else about Jay was little, and the azure kimono negligible. Naturally, he had my full attention.

"What *did* that sweet old fart say about me?"

He said you couldn't hit to left is what I wanted to say, wished I had said, because that's how Marsachino swung his way back into the minors. I'm sure Jay would have relished my smart mouth. (And maybe my new white sneakers from Sears.) Instead I stared. Perturbed, intrigued. Four years in the army and Burt was still leaving me at the doorstep.

"Don't look so shocked, baby. Come on in."

Baby? Where was Lancaster when I needed him?

I smiled involuntarily.

Not so Jay. He was far too sophisticated to move a muscle involuntarily, I supposed.

I stopped skittering the issue and settled my gaze on his kimono-colored eyes. Slits, trying to be tough and electrifying, but lonely and horny at forty is a telling combination, especially when witnessed by the young and ambitious. I glanced over his shoulder through the mirrored lamé foyer into the large white room, over and above a thousand stuffed pillows to the top-o'-the-heap picture window beyond. And I moved through that elegant doorway, one foot in front of the other, sideways, hugging the jamb, nudging filigree on my left, being oh-so-careful not to brush against a moving part on my right, for Jay refused to withdraw his generous invitation. Curious body, mind on the prowl, I walked through it all and directly to the picture window. Paramount lay below me and to the left, Fox to my right, Jay explained. I was aware that Warner's and Universal, where Jay was a big shot, hugged the brand-new Hollywood Freeway, but he told me anyway and I let him. At the moment, they flanked my rear, as did Jay.

"Baby, those jeans have *got* to go."

Lights began to pop on. All along the Sunset Strip.

"You look divine in yellow, but do launder that, what is it . . . cotton and what?" he asked himself, plucking the back of my sweatshirt. "At least half a dozen times before you even dream a dream of slipping it over those magnificent shoulders."

The town was in twilight. Open for business.

A naked man called me baby. Think of that.

What the hell. It was 1957.

I turned to Jay. "That sweet old fart said you were the premier costumer to the stars," I said in my best Barry Fitzgerald.

I'D NEVER tasted herb tea before.

I wanted to spit it back.

"Mmmm, good," I enthused. "Hot."

Jay Semple narrowed at the word hot, yet remained sprawled—a trick reserved for the short-waisted, I'm sure—and shot me a look from his clump of pillows across the miles to my clump, six feet and holding. A point of view that said he was going to straddle every syllable that fell out of my mouth that had the slightest tinge of sexual possibility, no matter how remote, and smirk me into submission.

I hadn't played that game since Dickie Greenberg and I sniggered our way through eighth grade hygiene. Miss Hecker, which rhymes with . . .

Eyes up! I said to myself. Fascinate yourself with his shiny little nubbin.

Avoid the statuary, principally the two-foot white ass on the piano. Don't ask him if he *plays.*

Ask him.

Can you help me, Mr. Semple? It's that simple.

Help me *what?* For I wasn't sure. I have so much fun at the movies. Never mind.

Shall I ask him now? Later by phone? Dash off a note?

I'll sock him. If he moves one giant iota in my direction. Right on top of his strange head is where I'll sock him. Wear this!

This zipper stays up.

They're baggy. So what?

Maybe we could go shopping.

"Boy, do you look a lot like Yul Brynner," I offered, warmly.

"Really?"

"Your head."

Had I done it again?

There was yes-yes in his eyes.

I lose, he wins, he goes directly to Cashier, and gets a free shake, thanks to the Virgin Mouth. What could I say? Certainly not *big, little, up, down*. Scratch any version of the verb *to lay*.

Jay was performing an autopsy on my jeans, and like it or not, I was a twisting labyrinth of innuendo.

Why not just accidentally dump this urn of piss on everything white that *sucks up* and knock his *ass* off the piano on my way out?

Take the train home.

Give Father Tiv a heart attack.

On the other hand, just shut the fuck up, I said to myself, finally.

And once again I took my attention over and above Jay's shoulder. Stood. Moved to the picture window. The motion picture window.

It was nice out there.

You can't hear the train like you can in Granville, but you can see Ciro's.

"You've got great eyes. Do you know that?" Jay said, joining me. It didn't sound like a real question. "I mean, do you really know it? Of course, the color's gorgeous. Everybody tells you that. But what intensity, my God, and you don't know it, do you?"

"Uh-uh." Let him decode that.

"You really don't, and that's why you're going to make it, baby." He put a hand on my shoulder and looked up at my face. "Because you've got it and don't know it."

I smiled at Jay and wondered if I'd lost something by not being John Wayne about the whole situation.

"Why so sad, baby?"

"Do you ever miss the train?"

"What train?"

"The S.P. through Granville."

"I'm here, baby."

"That's how I got here."

"I've arrived. One doesn't go back. More tea?"

"Half."

While Jay was refilling my urn—it was blue and white, streaks of yellow—I pondered the intensity of my eyes, tried to remember what I'd done to get them that way, and prepared to thank family and friends for all their help along the way.

"What in the world are you doing for dinner tonight?" Jay called from the kitchen.

I calculated MGM to be a little farther to the south-west, just out of sight.

"Who? Me?" I shrugged at the sky, which is the limit, they say. *The Sky's the Limit.* Fred Astaire said as much to Joan Leslie. I danced briefly with the air. "No plans."

JAY LOOKED more naked when he was fully clothed than he looked when he was fully naked.

"How about an after dinner drink? A little Galliano?" I knew what that was. (Ev made it from scratch one Labor Day weekend: water, grain alcohol, too much sugar. Aunt Rose said it made her teeth cry out in pain.) "Fernet Branca?" he further suggested.

Probably a magic potion.

Jay had been urged by nature to arrange his unit in an assemblage down his left trouser leg since he was eleven. He confided this to me over frozen daiquiris. And didn't I, for goodness sake, either wear myself down left or down right? Hard to believe. A *joint* he called it over chiffonade salad with house dressing. In toto: a *basket*. I chose the Welsh rarebit. Which I took to mean rabbit, and told him so, and he bathed me in his special look.

"What's Fernet Branca?" I ventured carefully.

"It's Italian, and it's *marvelous* for the tummy."

We sat in a red booth on the chic side of the Musso and Frank Grill, Hollywood's oldest, surrounded by denizens of the industry. Jay had spent part of the evening between anatomical meanderings identifying the larger assemblage. The Biz. Producers, directors, writers, actors, agents. Associate this, assistant that, and a whole lot of people who called a whole lot of other people baby. Obviously I was family.

"Hey, baby."

"Love ya, sweetheart."

"Call my service."

A tribal exchange I frequently overheard during my two unnecessary pilgrimages to the john and back, where I washed and rewashed my hands, enjoyed the towel machine, and twice reflected intensity. I was certain I saw Joan Collins exit the ladies' about the same time I noticed Mickey Rooney use his napkin.

Thankfully, the busboy swerved.

And gee, they were happy people, I observed, as I literally rubbed elbows and bumped shoulders, back and forth and forth and back. Everybody had a client and a studio and a hairstyle.

"What are you doing in there?" Jay asked, on my final trip across the room and into the booth. "Trolling?"

He was saying good night to a friend, en passant.

"We'll talk, baby."

"You're never home."

Call my service, I thought, an instant before Jay said it.

"What do you call it again?" I asked him.

"Fair-net Branc-a."

"I'll have that."

I was insatiable. Anything new and marvelous for the tummy sounded like a hell of an idea.

J AY SLID the Maserati up to the entrance of the Hollywood YMCA—several Maserati lengths ahead of it, actually—and toyed with his gear shift.

I clutched my door handle as if it were a gift from Jesus, and the instant the little bullet eased to a stop, I opened wide, planted one foot firmly onto Hudson Avenue, Hollywood, California, the other big white sneaker hopelessly dragging the decks of the *Niña, Pinta,* and *Santa Maria.* How does one say thanks and good night to a nudist as well as a cocksucker?

"I don't know how to thank you."

"Think of it as pussy on a stick," suggested Jay.

I had such a headache.

iii
· · ·

"So Jay sent'cha."

"Yes, sir."

"The feggela."

"Beg your pardon?"

"Ramona, honey, bring coffee. You want coffee?"

"That'd be fine, thanks."

"Coca-Cola?"

"Coffee is fine."

"Black?"

"Swell."

"We got tea, you want tea, and don't call me sir. What do I look like, an alta cocker?* Relax, call me Stan. How da hell old are you, anyway?"

"Twenty-four, Stan."

"Don't lie to me."

"Honest."

*Very old guy

· 28 ·

"Ya don't look it. You could go maybe nineteen, twenty tops. So. Pisher.* Ya wanna be an actor. Ya don't got enough problems? Who cuts your hair, your mother?"

"Too short?"

"Too square. Drink, while it's hot. Sangenito, huh? Br-o-o-o-no Sangenito, what da hell kind of a name is that?"

"It's Italian."

"No shit, I thought it was Chinese. Hey, no aspersions. It's got no balls for da business is what I'm sayin'. No reflection. You want sugar? So the feggela tells me on the phone, this kid's got a great pair of eyes. Right, eyes! But to myself I say *hock mir nisht kin chaynick.*† Am I right? You want sugar?"

"Probably."

"Take sugar. I mean, who sees Clint Walker's eyes, for chrissake? He squints. Like this, he squints."

"Have you ever met Burt Lancaster?" I asked.

"He sees me in the commissary, we wave. You wanna know who had eyes? Eyes that could knock ya on your ass? You don't remember her."

"Who?"

"Christina Corday. Before your time."

"I remember her."

"Bullshit."

"I do."

---

*Very young guy
†Don't bust my kishkas.

"Bullshit."

"Rhythm on the Ranch."

"No!"

"Yeah!"

"You remember that? Ya hadda be . . ."

"Five."

"No shit?"

"And nine months. My very first movie ever."

"No shit."

"No shit. At the El Rey, back in Granville. I remember everything: Buck Jones, Humphrey Bogart, Dick Powell . . ."

"In your wildest dreams, who da hell you think got her that gig for good bread and third billing under Rudy Vallee?"

"Stan?"

"Emmis."*

"Emmis?"

"Would I lie? *Desert Rose, Countess from Flatbush* . . . shit, I handled Christina for years, till she went to da Morris office. What da hell, water under da dam. Br-o-o-o-no Sangenito, huh? Amazing you remember her. Listen, boychik†, the business is fucked. Talent don't mean shit no more. I can't promise bupkis‡, but ya got a nice quality, so you'll get a haircut and bring me some eight-by-ten

*No shit
†Sonny
‡Nada

glossies, and maybe I'll send ya to meet some people. We don't put nothin' on paper. Know what her name was when I found her? Alice Shragowitz awreddy."

"She wore a cowboy hat and played the ukelele."

"A zeesa maydel* by any other name."

WHAT DID it all mean?

I wondered, as I sauntered out of the Stanley Feinberg Agency and stepped into the elevator, with rather a nice quality, I thought, and eventually wandered west, upstream toward the famous Pantages Theatre—NOW PLAY-ING: *Twelve Angry Men.* Over to Hollywood and Vine, where I hung around and didn't see a soul I knew, except for maybe one starlet. Anyway, she could have been.

Where did they all hang out?

Everybody.

Up to Frederick's of Hollywood. It was sunny and warm. I loitered the area. Bought the best pair of sunglasses. Made another pass.

I scoured side streets, hating the necessary detour. Found a Laundromat with nobody in it, just regular people, and washed my sweatshirt only three times because I ran out of nickels for the dryer and was too embarrassed to ask for change with my shirt off.

I studied Grauman's Chinese. The sidewalk outside.

They weren't there. Burt Lancaster's footprints weren't

*Nice girl

even there. I wouldn't see a movie at the Chinese if you paid me.

Found a pair of shades I liked better—darker, blacker—bought those, too, bit off the tag, broke the first pair and dumped them.

"What's an eight-by-ten glassy?" was only one of the urgent questions I wrote down in my small blue spiral notebook from Lee's Drugs and asked Jay from the safety of a toasty phone booth at Coffee Dan's on big, wide, wonderful Hollywood Boulevard.

"*Glossy*, silly! Eight-by-ten glossy!"

God, what a sketch I was, and how marvelously naive. Publicity pictures were a must, and by all means, do hustle my tight little ass over to Jay Sebring's for a style.

Another Jay. For twenty bucks. Some style.

Meantime, not to worry, Ritchie to the rescue. Little Ritchie Rembrandt, who's caca cheap if one knows the right people, and he'll *adore* shooting me if they're still speaking after the other night. Make me look *divine* for my head shots.

Naive, my tight little ass.

Shut up, I should have said. For five minutes. I know what I need. Practical stuff. An apartment smack-dab in the heart of the matter. And a car. A date with Deborah Kerr in the crashing surf is what I need. Not necessarily a Maserati.

And a job, we agreed. A shit-job, Jay said, not a job-job. So I can be free. To pursue my career. To go to lunch and meet sophisticated people. Have interviews and auditions, and maybe even a screen test someday. Not now, but soon.

No maybes about it.

Wasn't that Henry Fonda I noticed eating scrambled eggs at the counter?

No, but close.

iv

...

"**I** know that guy," Margie said, indicating the bar area.

Ports was filling up.

"Which guy?"

Again without looking, a tilt of the head. "Him."

"The bartender?"

"Yeah."

"You know the bartender?"

"Uh-huh."

I smiled. "From Fresno?"

"He's in the movies."

How marvelously naive, I thought.

"Yeah, some dumb commercial. On the beach, balancing all those bathing beauties. Budweiser. Anyway, he's not my type. Too young."

I upended my glass and pondered smugness till my ice cubes hit me in the mouth.

Margie wrinkled her nose. "And too much goddamn hair." A minimum of disgust.

What else could I do but excuse myself, jump up, and move in good fellowship to the bar? All of us at the asylum enjoy the warmth of recognition now and then. One of the reasons we kicked the door in in the first place—Jerry had a quality, no question about it—and locked it behind us and swallowed the key.

"Mazel tov,* Jerry," I stated pretty sincerely. "On the Bud"—Irish grin, pushing thirty, too many teeth—and gave him a good whack on his ripply arm. For which we got a Scotch and a bourbon on the house.

"He's not as cute as you," said Margie on my return. "Not nearly. Neither was Skeets Klitgaard for that matter."

Skeets Klitgaard?

"*You* should have been Li'l Abner."

"Li'l who?"

"At the Sadie Hawkins Day Dance."

Jesus.

"Especially *me* being Daisy Mae."

How do I end this?

"And *him* being a blond and all."

Let me count the ways.

"A measly seventy-three votes. Imagine. How come I never see you in a commercial?"

*Congratulations

"Charmin," I mumbled. And sank. Not much, just a little.

"I never saw it."

"So squeezably soft it's irresistible?"

"How come I never saw it?"

I recalled being hidden behind a six-foot roll of toilet paper. "How's your drink?" I answered.

"A helluva lot better'n the last one. I'd have remembered," she added, and touched my hand as I lit her cigarette. Her fingernails were short. A typist, probably. And simply done.

"It was a while back."

Margie lifted her eyes and seared me with gravity through flame. "I'd have remembered."

Perry Como belted "Prisoner of Love."

I SURE as heck wasn't about to break the news during *From Here to Eternity*, although I'd already seen it twice, both times at the El Rey.

I'd wait.

Not at the creamery, either.

Later, in the car after we necked.

Probably.

Or before.

No, after.

As long as she didn't bury her head in her hands like she did when Frank Sinatra and Montgomery Clift got killed. Or sob out loud. I couldn't stand that. For instance, when Deborah Kerr threw her lei off the ship and into the ocean and it floated out to sea, which meant for sure they'd never see each other again. Personally, I just stare at the head in front of me and think about the Brooklyn Dodgers. Donna Reed was no slouch, either.

"Maybe they get together, finally," I explained on the drive back to Margie's house. "I mean, maybe she comes back to Hawaii one day and he's still there and agrees to go to officers' school. I know: maybe he gets stationed in the States and they run into each other on the street or something. Or maybe . . ."

Happy endings pooped out about the time I turned off the headlights and the motor *before* coming to a complete stop so we wouldn't wake anybody up and homecoming would remain forever a mystery. The first time I tried it I hit the curb and the horn and almost ruined my life. And woke up half the neighborhood, including Margie's mother, who I wouldn't dream of disturbing.

We sat there for a minute. Quietly. You can hear the drizzle hit the windshield on Baywood Avenue after dark.

Part of me wanted to just blurt it out.

Not yet, I said to myself.

"I liked the part best when they were on the beach at night and the waves kept rolling over them," I said out loud, softly to the dashboard.

Margie was staring at the dash, too. I could tell out of the corner of my eye. She kind of cooed, "Yeahhhh," a little on the husky side. Which seemed like an ideal time to put my arm around her pink angora shoulders, because one never knows. If the timing isn't perfect, you're not sure whether to get on with it or say something stupid, or just listen to your heart till your arm falls off.

We sat there and watched two pieces of drizzle race to the hood. Fascinating.

On the other hand, if a person sits in the dark long enough, quietly enough, he begins to have memories about the way things ought to be. A happy ending, or no ending at all.

So I kissed her on the lips. Softly. We moved together at exactly the same time for once in my life. Very softly at first because we prefer it that way, at her suggestion.

My pimple was killing me.

Soon we were breathing through our noses.

I wondered for a split second if Deborah Kerr put her tongue in Burt Lancaster's mouth. Just for a split second. And darted it around like that. Of course. And him, too. And took it back and put it in and took it back.

Was it a hook or a snap or a clasp? "I can't . . . how do I . . . I can't . . . find it . . ." Was it in front? How I loved her. I wedged my hand up underneath her angora. How soft. Last time it was in front . . .

"In back," she whispered. She loved me, too, I could tell, although she didn't say it in so many words. I buried my face into her sweet neck and bit, not much, just a little, and she made noises like nobody makes in the movies. "There . . . no . . . don't pull it . . . no, the other way . . . the *other* way . . ." Not at all impatient. I was impatient, never Margie. How did she get that way? Like a polite soldier sometimes. "Here, let me," she said, and didn't even look up. A quick maneuver, a little shrug, and her brassiere was under her chin. Last time I'd pulled it down underneath, half-staff, half-assed, and they were all scrunched up at attention.

At ease.

I brushed her with my lips and put her in my mouth, as much as humanly possible, and the steering wheel was killing my back, but hardly a factor. Her nipples were like little hard dicks, I thought for a split second—a very split second—obviously, everything I was doing was immoral, yet the whole world smelled of Would You.

"Oh, God, oh, God," she murmured, over and over again, almost like a warning, as the skin inside her knee came to me like smooth frosting, and slowly I finger-crept to the inside of her thigh. We preferred it that way, I could tell, even though it was the first time. "Ohhhh, God . . ."

Would she touch me? Ever in a million years? Now? It's a zipper. Here, let me? I wondered as I wandered to discover tufts of angel fur, wet and warm and light and heavy, slipping, shoving against my fingers. Angora America.

"Ohhhhhhh, God," she moaned.

I love you, I love you. I told her so much. It was wild on my mind. Here let me—

"Stop!"

"Huh?"

"Stop."

"Stop?"

"Please."

"Now?"

"Now."

"Why?"

"We can't."

"I want to, I want to."

"I know," Margie admitted, as she attempted to fold her hands on her lap, while mine were still in the vicinity.

"Please?" I tried not to whine.

"Not unless we're going to get married."

"Married?" I asked, leaving the vicinity.

"Yes. And even then we should wait."

So we did. We moved, each to our own private side of the Plymouth. And waited, and waited . . .

"You said you loved me."

And waited . . .

"I do."

"Don't you want to marry me, then?"

"Well, sure. Look how we fogged up the windows. Someday. Sure."

"What do you mean, *someday*?"

"I mean . . . I just . . . I mean, I can't make any long range plans, that's all . . . because . . . because . . ." I started to draw something on my window. A heart. "I joined the army."

"The *army*?"

"Shhhh, you'll wake your mom."

"The army?"

"Yesterday."

I told her everything, while she stared at her window. I explained in great detail that I wasn't sure what I wanted to do with my life. That in the first place, my grades weren't that hot, and in the second place, I'd been influenced lately to join up. Maybe even have a career. Maybe eventually even go to officers' school, I explained to the back of her head. I told her almost everything.

"I've gotta go in."

"Wait a minute . . ."

"I've gotta go." She touched the door handle.

"Don't just leave like that."

"It's late. I'm gonna catch holy hell."

"What're you so mad about? We'll see each other. Like when I'm on leave and stuff, and I'll write every day. I promise."

She looked at me with small eyes I'd never seen before. "What the hell am I supposed to do while you're away? Twiddle my thumbs?" Then back to the window. "And what if you get killed or something?"

"I won't." I couldn't believe she said hell twice in the same night, the same minute.

"I don't want to see you anymore." She fixed her brassiere. I wanted to help.

"I won't get killed. I don't have to leave for a month."

"I'm going inside."

"Let me walk you to the door."

"Don't bother."

"Please."

She opened the door. I could smell the eucalyptus.

"I love you," I said. "Honest."

She didn't slam it. Just made sure it was closed.

A flower lei is supposed to float back to shore, I should have said. *That's the point.* I watched her march, shoulders slumped a little, which I'd never noticed before, up the cement path to a drummer I'd never heard.

I expected her to cry at least a little bit, so I could take her in my arms and kiss away her tears. Halt, who goes there? I thought for a split second.

NO ONE appears as gigantic as Burt Lancaster in starched khakis and sergeant stripes.

"*Watch it, kid!*"

"*Huh?*"

"*You just missed a tree.*"

"*I did?*"

"*Big sycamore. And took us through a stop sign a block south of Baywood.*" He smiled, the way he did before Pearl Harbor. "*Sailed us right through, nice as you please.*"

"*Sorry, sir.*"

"*Park the car.*"

"*I'm fine.*"

"*That's an order, kid. Get used to it.*"

So I did. I want to be tough, I thought.

"*A tough guy, huh?*"

"A hero. Like you."

"I get it."

"Instead of how I am."

"How are you, kid?"

"Fine . . . sir!"

"You're not fine."

"I am."

"You're not. You got a kick in the teeth back there. Cry it out."

"Tough guys don't cry."

"That's where you're wrong."

"Name me one."

"You saw Marlon Brando twice in—"

"You're tougher than him."

"That's beside the point. You're cryin' this very minute."

"I'm not."

"You are. Inside, where it hurts most. Now hear me and hear me good." I could swear he had a broken beer bottle in his fist. *"Let it out. Let it out big. Otherwise the pain lays inside your gut forever and rots it out, as sure as I'm sittin' here. That's it. Thaaat's it. Let 'er rip. Now listen to me, kid. This ain't the end of the world. It ain't the end of the pain, either, 'cuz pain's got a way of hangin' around a lot longer than we plan on it. But the worst is over, hear me? And one day you're gonna wake up in the morning and the sun'll be shinin' through your window to beat the band, and layin' its warmth all over the covers, and you'll be healed. Start the car. I'll take the wheel."*

I heard a train whistle at the Edgemont crossing. It was too early for the Daylight, too late for the Lark.

"This ain't your last kick in the teeth, kid. Mark my words. Have I ever steered you wrong?"

A slow freight, probably, going who knows where.

V

· · ·

Granville, California
June, 1953

Hi, Honey,

. . . Ye gods, it sure wasn't easy getting all that angora off your nice yellow cashmere I bought you,
but never mind. A pain in the you know what!
Ha. Ha. It's time for you to have fun, now, do
you hear me? *Fun!!!* Charles agrees and says hi.
Tonight we're going to watch *The Colgate Comedy
Hour* . . .

Love, Ev (Mom)

Fort Ord, California
July, 1953

Dear Ev,

. . . It's very foggy here, and I keep closing the
wrong eye when I shoot my M-1, which is a ri-
fle . . .

Granville, California
August, 1953

Hi, Sweetie,
. . . Congratulations on being accepted to clerical
school. Charles says it's a darn good thing the
war is over. I can't argue with that. Keeping my
fingers crossed for Hawaii . . .

Guam has warm weather most of the year. Temperatures
range from seventy-two to eighty-eight. Captain Pheiffer
is from Monroe, Louisiana, and has eyes like bullet holes
in a redwood tree. He caught me being James Cagney in
The Fighting 69th, jumping on a live grenade on my bunk
one Sunday when the barracks were quiet. Magellan discovered Guam in 1521 A.D. His wife wears sundresses
with heels and no stockings. Captain Pheiffer says if every soldier was like me, the national language would be
Chippewa. Marie Rosario says I'm premature.

ADAK, ALASKA, on the other hand, is probably the
southernmost island in the Aleutian chain. Sergeant Tolliver from Paducah, Kentucky, caught me being him in
the mirror in the latrine and says if I were kin to him,
he'd shoot me for treason—and it's a good thing I can
type seventy-five words a minute. Having second thoughts
about officers' school. No wonder his wife is unhappy. He
says if my head was any farther up my ass, I'd be smiling
upside down at my shoelaces. I see her at the PX.

"I don't know who I am. One false move and
I'm yours."

The Cocoanuts
PARAMOUNT PICTURES, 1929

vi
. . .

It was business as usual at Baskin Robbins 31 Flavors
when Doris Day ambled in for five gallons of rocky
road. She told somebody, "Don't tell me what I
want, Marty," and actually smiled at me. I wish she'd
walked out the door with me instead of him. Van John-
son asked me very seriously where I was from and what
in the world I was doing in Hollywood. "Keep your left
up, kid." He prefers cherry vanilla by the cone. Rod
Steiger is a big butter pecan man, and told me as much.
I hated wearing the little white hat.

Walt taught me how to make a scoop look like a flower
with practically no ice cream in the center. Chintzy, I
thought, at seventeen cents a cone. "We don't want nobody leavin' us in the lurch to become a movie star, ha,
ha, ha," he told me the day he hired me. When he wasn't
looking, I developed the Sangenito scoop, made forty-
eight bucks a week, and just yesterday bumped into Jack

Lemmon and asked him for directions I didn't need on my way to Film Fan Foto to pick up my eight-by-ten glossies.

It was only a matter of time.

"You're not *aware* of Ravel's Bolero?" Ritchie Rembrandt had asked, as if I'm supposed to be an expert on everything all of a sudden. "The sex act set to music, silly! Don't tell me that's news to Bruno Sangenito's ears?"

He used both names. They do that here. ("*Hi*, Bruno Sangenito!") As if on sight he solved some big mystery about me that hadn't quite come to the surface. He also wore capped sleeves. *Her thing* according to Jay, who God knows, had a thing of his own—so it was hardly a shock, and neither was Ritchie's little apartment in West Hollowood, which looked exactly like a Port Said whorehouse—wherever in the world that is—Jay was right as rain once more. Torrential beaded curtains.

"Definitely the sex act," Ritchie repeated, regarding me through the camera around his neck.

"It's nice. I never heard it before."

Music to my ears was the closest I'd come to a thing of my own since I'd ejaculated into the New World.

Prematurely?

Nah.

"Definitely," Ritchie mumbled.

It was eleven A.M. We sipped white wine and listened to a concert, I guess you'd call it.

"Care for a joint?" He passed it from his easy chair toward my tall stool in the center of the room.

"Noooo, thank you."

"Soooo relaxing."

And I wondered what that world within my world was all about. No point in getting toooo relaxed, however. I knew what *I* wanted as well, had practiced as much the night before. A look here, a leer there, till the bathroom mirror finally made sense of it all.

Time passed.

I leered.

He stared.

"Something's missing." He jumped up. "What on earth could it be?" Circled me three times. "Lose the sunglasses, baby," he suggested with a trailing hand and a look that said he was sorry, and disappeared behind the beads.

Burst out.

Whipped to parade rest in front of my stool, twinkled, and with no coaxing from me, very quickly produced: The Hat.

Black. Rough leather band. Studs poking out all over the place. A hint of trail dust.

And jammed it onto my head. Squinched it down. Pulled away. Chin in hand. Back again, squinch.

"Ow." *Gunfight at the O.K. Corral.*

"Shall we take it from the middle?" Ritchie asked, and moved to the phonograph and back again in a hop skip.

"Ride 'em cowboy!"

. . . *Tum-ta-da-da-dum* . . .

Click.

"Yes!"

. . . *Ta-da-da-dum* . . .

Click.

"Yes!"

Click, click, yes, yes.

Yes, yes, click.

. . . *Ta-da-da-dum* . . . *Wheeeeeeeee* . . . *doodee-doodee-doodee* . . .

"Yes!"

. . . *Bum-bum-bum-bum* . . .

"God!"

Boom!

CLICK!

"YES!"

Wheeeeeeeee. . . .

I SAID a definite no to the sailor pants with half the buttons ripped off, and was glad of it. And a definite no to the chain mail. Who the hell does he think I am? Imagine me wielding a mace.

Tarzan was a horse of a different color, I decided again and again as I leapt into the elevator, pictures in hand.

There have been exactly twenty-one Tarzan movies

made to date, with six different Tarzans, counting talkies alone. "This town is forever looking for Tarzans," Ritchie explained. I had the perfect body, it seemed to him, and he had the spear and the loincloth right behind the beads. No extra charge.

What the hell.

He flatly refused to sell me The Hat. "I worship at the feet of this fucking hat."

"Oy!"* Stan's head was in his hands. He was talking to his desk. "Oy! Never again a three martini lunch! Which I should know awreddy from past experience. Hand 'em over, hand 'em over. Ramona, bring coffee, honey, and a bicarbonate. Oy! What do I see lookin' up at me here?"

"It's me."

"Allow me to be the judge." He sat back in his chair, swirled a quarter of a turn in order to get the best possible light from the window behind him. He examined each photo and one by one carpeted his desktop. "Uh-huh . . . uh-huh . . . uh-huh . . . What da fuck is *this*?"

"No extra charge."

"Thank God. Uh-huh . . . uh-*huh*. Ya know what I see?"

"Uh-uh."

"I'll tell ya what I see. Ramona, honey, come back, whadda *you* see? At first glance. An honest opinion."

*Oy

Ramona studied the spread, then she studied me, then she studied Stan.

"What the hell does she know?" he said to the wall. "And call the Cock'n Bull. Tell 'em find my glasses before somebody sits on 'em. Ya wanna know what I see? I'll tell ya what I see. Menace! Emmis! Either that or the hat don't fit. I sure as hell don't see no Br-o-o-o-no Sanja-whatever-da-hell lookin' up at me. I'll tell ya what's lookin' up at me. Bruno . . . what? Bruno Adams, Adam Bruno, Bruno something, something Bruno, Bruno boom-boom, boom-boom Bruno, I got a headache awreddy. Larry, Harry, Barry, Jimmy, Johnny Bruno. Johnny Bruno." Stanley Feinberg tilted his head upward. His eyes scoured the ceiling and presently glistened with revelation. "A fuckin' Johnny Bruno, thaaat's what's lookin' up at me tellin' me ta go fuck myself under that hat! A *Johnny*-fuckin'-*Bruno!*" He smiled at me. "Ya happy?"

I bounced a little on the balls of my feet.

"*This* here picture," Stan advised, "you should put by you in the pocket and find yourself a nice girl named Jane. Abee gazunt, Mr. Johnny Bruno, which you should know means remain healthy till next we meet. Ya get my drift?"

vii

. . .

Theodore Drieser was a writer—*An American Tragedy*—I looked it up. The best thing about living in my little apartment above the garage on the old Theodore Drieser estate is that the Daisy Fresh juice bar is only fifty-seven steps away, and my next door neighbor is Jane Wyatt—*Father Knows Best*—who even though she's very sophisticated, trims her own lawn. She wears glasses and garden gloves and always has something pleasant to say every time I saunter by. I always say, "Good morning, Mrs. Ward," which is her real name. She doesn't know mine from Adam because I've come to the conclusion that I'm basically shy no matter what my name is.

The Daisy Fresh is run by two Belgian ladies.

"Bonjour, Monsieur Zjonnie Bruno!"

"Bonjour, Finette. Bonjour, Irene!"

"Bonjour, bonjour!"

Never in Granville.

The Raincheck Room is a mere three hundred and six-teen steps from my apartment, not counting the thirteen stairs, taken one at a time, heading up to my front door, another legitimate one and a half on the landing, and the additional nine to the bathroom mirror. Three hundred thirty-nine and a half in all.

Einstein, I thought, as I wondered why I bothered counting at all while I sipped my umpteenth Schlitz. Or why the most beautiful girls in the world, each in her own right a Miss America and probably very nice if they'd ever give a person a chance to get acquainted, suddenly become fascinated by something vague at the other end of the bar every time I try my level best to introduce Johnny-fuckin' Bruno to West Hollywood. Same at Barney's Beanery. Who cares how many steps? And the Arrow Market and Peter's Cleaners and Dominic's Deli-catessen, a personal favorite. I've seen *Love in the God-damn Afternoon* three times already, as Stan would say, and I practically live in *The Rainmaker*.

"The name you choose for yourself is more your own than the name you were born with!" the savage in me says to Katharine Hepburn. *"Dream you're somebody,"* he contin-ues. No wonder I rarely speak. *"Be somebody!"*

"Phil, may I have another, please?"

The other night I lit somebody's hair. Zippo, and that was that.

"Thanks, Phil. Busy tonight."

I have yet to plunge into the beckoning jaws of death by knocking my glass over, but the possibility throttles my fingers every time I hoist one to say, "Hi!" or something equally colorful. Margie Cosgrove. God. Jay says I'm ballsy. Easy for him. What if she walked in the door right now? He also confided to me that no is the sexiest word in Hollywood.

"Some crowd, hey Phil?"

For instance, Miss Tallest Blonde in the World without exaggeration on the stool to my immediate right, whose reflection I've been eating off the mirror behind the bar and whose ponytail is practically wending its way up my nostrils, has yet to give me a tumble.

"I beg your pardon?" she said, flipping my way.

"I was just saying to Phil that the place is really jammed tonight."

"Do you always make obvious statements?"

"May I buy you a drink?"

"My friend's in the rest room."

In a pissing contest with *The Rainmaker* no doubt.

I THOUGHT ABOUT calling home as I ambled west on Santa Monica Boulevard. I turned left at the Daisy Fresh, crossed the street, and spent some time looking in the window of Berman's Costume Shop, where I'd tried on several hats the day before and pretended. I crossed the street onto King's Road, turned left, and at the forty-seventh or forty-eighth step—I can't recall which—I marched right into the trunk of Mrs. Ward's enormous tree near the curb and hit the ground and didn't know where I was for a split second. I figured, as long as I'm on my ass, I might as well cry it out.

Who am I?

I wondered.

The moment I arrived at my apartment I opened a can of Spam and summoned memories of leg of lamb with mint jelly and crispy potatoes just the way I like it.

After a late supper, I saw myself in the mirror as the only Capricorn usher at the El Rey with an eight-by-ten glossy and a Sebring cut, Pisces rising.

It was definitely too late to call home.

viii
• • •

I'd been cleaning my *surps*. That's what Walt calls them. "Your chocolate, your strawberry, your butterscotch surps." And contemplating my tomorrows and hating my little white hat.

And yanked it. And stuffed it under the register.

Not coincidentally . . .

At the very instant a certain Miss Dusty Germaine slinked through the door to an otherwise empty palace of many flavors fifteen minutes before closing. Ten forty-five precisely.

She wore a black cocktail dress similar to the one Jay had designed for Zsa Zsa Gabor, or so he said—everybody steals, Jay says—with spaghetti straps, and looked as if her parents owned a state back east.

She put an extraordinary fingernail to her lips and dawdled over the ices, which are very much like your sherbet, but no butterfat. Also quite close to the front door, I realized immediately as I attempted to move catlike the length of the counter, tripped only once where the runners don't meet—mustn't lose her company to an afterthought. Checked my style. Whistled the sex act lightly between my teeth, up-tempo, thought briefly of Sergeant Tolliver's wife, for which I forgive myself constantly, and occasionally hit myself over the head, though not literally, for I looked "Mighty invitin' " at the PX, said Mitzi Tolliver, but "Premature as all get out, not to worry, there's a first time for everything, 'bye, sweet thing."

In any event, I swiveled into position.

"What'll it be?" Nice as you please.

And stared. Down into the upraised face of Miss Dusty Germaine over ice, and recognized her immediately as the flavor of substance most often between my body and the stained sheets where I live in the American Tragedy.

We moved together, slink for slink, did Dusty and I, she on her side of the counter, I on mine—scrutinizing thirty-one options, ta-da-da-dum. I deftly overcame the gap where the runners don't meet.

Had she been to a party?

The Philadelphia Story at Ava Gardner's house, I surmised.

She paused at the butter brickle.

"What's *your* favorite flavor?" Not at all in a quandary.

"Lime ice," I lied, avoiding vanilla.

"Sounds scrumptious."

"No butterfat."

"Make it a double."

"Flat cone or pointy?"

"Pointy."

"You're on."

"I'm Dusty."

Was I dreaming it all?

No.

"I'm Bruno."

Here.

"Hi, Bruno."

At the ready.

"Hi, Dusty."

"Dusty *Germaine*," she breathed as she accepted my cone and I refused her money with narrowed eyes. Had our fingers touched briefly during the exchange?

"*Hi*, Dusty Germaine!"

I couldn't say anything wrong.

For a change.

Finally.

But decided not to press my luck, and in the ensuing moments confined my remarks to a crooked grin as I watched her lick and move in liquid measure among the pink and brown polka dots.

She'd left the party early, it turned out. So many dull people, such a hot night. Scoured the west side, hungry for something. She wasn't sure what.

"A nightcap?"

Sweet Smell of Success, I thought, for presently the world reduced itself, and smacked of soft leather, rich perfume, and cocktails well-spent. The Mercedes Benz 190 SL, it turned out, creamy blue, made its way up Cañon Drive, through the flats, jogged neatly to the left on Sunset, nicely to the right and farther up. Up rapidly at first, then slowly squiggled every which way into the hidden tributaries of Benedict Canyon.

I scrunched toasty in the passenger seat, as lady moon played an on-again, off-again chiaroscuro on the aristocratic knees of Miss Dusty Germaine.

Gee, I thought, this is what the hell it's all about.

"Dynamite pictures, acceptable focus," Ritchie had said, which I took to mean perfect. The Hat did the trick, though somewhat low at the brim, "We *assume* the scheme in those big hazel eyes."

"Watch me," Dusty whispered. "Stay by the fire and watch me."

The carpet was fathomless, a shade lighter than the fawn upholstery that got us there. The fireplace was a hall closet on its side.

"Lie there. Don't move," she said, as she swung to the far far side of the room along with the Misty Miss June Christy, who just happened to be warbling from the console. *This Time the Dream's on Me.*

Cognac by Rémy.

She stood. Faced me. Slowly placed her snifter on the carpet, and on the way up, oopsie-daisy, gathered the hem of the Zsa Zsa and moved it right along with her, nice as you please, up, up, and over—hardly snagging an earring. The dress sailed across the room in my direction. A chandelier-high change-up that dropped helplessly within an inch of my vicinity.

"Watch me."

Yes, yes, click, click.

And she teased, as a feather duster teases. Here, there, subtle on the outside, barely on the inside, around and in between. Nylon and silk sank to the carpet in ribbons of gift wrap.

"Oh, baby . . . Oh, baby . . ."

Is it me, Jesus?

No, my son. She giveth to she.

But soft!

Be my guest.

Be your guest.

Do wend over soon to my side of the room, however . . .

Stay there.

Come soon.

Finally . . .

Smoothly . . .

Dusty the Duster swept my way like the big second hand on a Seth Thomas clock.

I helped with my clothes the best that I could, till together we arrived at my jockeys from Sears. She slapped me off course, took her very long time . . .

To discover . . .

By happenstance?

Uncover . . .

"If you come, I'll kill you." And spoke to me in tongues.

Jamoca fudge, jamoca fudge . . .

Then slipped me inside. Backed off and moved in, backed off and moved in . . .

Ja-mo-ca . . .

"Now . . . *Nowwwwww!*" She jerked and she twisted, and ordered us around.

" CALL ME ," she whispered as she dropped me in silence and darkness, very near the who am I tree. "Promise?"

ix

. . .

Ports was awash with sex appeal, three deep at the bar.

"Try and get 'em to smile for a picture!" Margie harrumphed as we flipped through plastic folder after plastic folder, the kids and exes and the stepfathers and kids of kids. "This is Kimberlee . . ."

We leaned toward one another, four elbows on the table.

"Uh-huh . . ."

"My youngest. Actually, she's much cuter 'n that."

"Uh-*huh*."

"And Sandy . . ."

"Poor Sandy, having a bad day, no doubt," I offered, and could have shot myself, although the gang did have a singularity of focus.

"And Harvey and his kids, Sharon and Sally . . ."

"Twins?"

"Nah, they just look alike."

Had they been wrenched from the TV in the den, perhaps?

"And Kevin . . ."

Coaxed at gunpoint off the Ponderosa?

"And Debbie . . . she's full of hell, but you'd never know it."

Hustled up and bound and gagged for a split second of unbridled bliss?

"And Joey. He's got something in his mouth."

"Quite a family."

"And the son of a bitch in the picture with him owes me about fifty thousand in back child support."

Jesus, I was tired.

"Can we have another drink?"

And wishy-washy.

"Why not?"

Yet determined.

"One more and we're history," I assured Jerry after arriving at the bar, having cut my way through a herd of arms and legs and clustered youth. "Cut, print, save the arc."

"Cut to the chase?" suggested Jerry.

Not a chance, I indicated. A weary cock of the head, a roll of the eyes.

"Do you think you could send me some autographed pictures for my kids?" Margie rifled her smallish purse.

"Sure," I said, chin in hand, elbow on table, on the brink of largesse.

"Big ones with Johnny Bruno on them? Y'know, best wishes and stuff?"

"Happy to."

She withdrew a felt-tipped pen, located a nearly dry cocktail napkin, and soaked it with names: the Rorschach six.

"And send me one, okay? Just for me?"

"Okay."

We drank in unison.

"And write something on it."

"Absolutely!"

"Besides best wishes, I mean."

And continued to do so.

"Gee, I love this place!"

"It loves you."

"*What's* it called?"

"Ports. Spelled backwards, *strop*." I smiled. "Anagramical of *rsopt*," I added, and they say I can't play comedy.

"My best friend, Geneva, has a picture of Charles Bronson in her bedroom of all places."

"He's not as cute as me."

A.k.a. Bruno Sangenito had a little buzz in his head.

"Ha! You can say that again!"

As did Margie Cosgrove.

"Skits Kleetgaard either, for that matter. Whatever happened to old Skeets?"

"I haven't seen that jerk since the Sadie Hawkins Day Dance."

"Sales, probably."

"Not once."

"You did."

"What?"

"See him."

"When?"

"The parking lot."

"Ha!"

"Back of the Ad. Building."

"You remember that?"

"After the rally for the Hartnell game."

"Ha! All he ever wanted was to get up my skirt."

"How's your mom?" I asked, hardly changing the subject.

"My mom? Oh, she's dead."

As if to say, she's in Detroit.

"Oh, no."

As if to say, let's bring her out to the coast. . . .

Margie grabbed a cigarette, lit up without assistance, exhaled bluntly at the near wall. "Yeah. Way back in the Sixties."

"Oh, no."

And ask her to sit and buy her a drink and light her a Lucky . . .

"Lung cancer."

"Jesus."

And say, hi, Beryl. May I call you Beryl?

"She thought you were the greatest thing since sliced bread."

And thanks.

"Do you remember . . . ?" we asked, somehow simultaneously.

Of course. Her smile. She was forever smiling, and so interested in everything, and those freckles, oh my yes, and the amber glasses—you remember that? Oh, my, yes, and how abashed I was the day I swung madly with my 7Up bottle to answer her. God knows what question she'd posed as we stood, the three of us, in terrible proximity near the fridge, and I chipped your tooth, and she kept repeating that it was only an accident, and accidents happen, as she looked at me and touched my arm. Not to worry. Tall, wasn't she? For those days. Five-six, that's all? But of course three-inch heels make all the difference in the world.

"See?" Margie strongly indicated the corner of her right front tooth. "Right here." If a finger could swagger. "She thought you were a real sweetheart."

So were we all, and whatever happened to those, I wondered as I reached across the table and took her hand and couldn't resist kissing it once and holding it against my face purposefully.

Margie reclaimed, wiped dampness from her eyes with her sleeve. "Would you like a picture of me?"

Of course.

"Here, this is for you," she offered, handing me a small white envelope. A two-by-three glossy? In a way. There was a roaring fire—that much was clear—and a pair of white shorts, legs posed sideways, of course, and together. Was it a happy face? Hard to tell on that big bear rug, in the buzz and dimness of Ports. Either Margie Cosgrove, I thought, or Loretta Young.

Acceptable focus.

"You haven't changed a bit," I said.

"Life's never quite interesting enough, somehow. You people who come to the movies know that."

The Matchmaker
PARAMOUNT PICTURES, 1958

X
. . .

BEGINNERS—EXPLORE THE JOYS OF ACTING WITH PHOEBE SAX is what the sign at the Daisy Fresh kept bellowing down at me from the bulletin board during who knows how many egg salad specials, along with a phone number which I finally transcribed onto a matchbook from the Raincheck just to make me feel better.

Every once in a while I get the yen to put the top down on the Mercedes and take a nice long drive all the way out Sunset Boulevard, beginning just below the Strip—corner Fairfax, Thrifty Drug, which is not where Sunset begins, but where it rises to the occasion. Schwab's makes the second best chicken soup I've ever tasted. I like it best when Loma serves it. Everybody knows Loma. I'm getting so I nod at the guys at the counter. Apple pie at Googies, corner Crescent Heights. Mona is by far the friendliest. James Dean used to hang out, she says.

On the other hand, who ever heard of Phoebe Sax?

Once in a while I get the urge to weave through Beverly Hills and wind around Brentwood—count cars? I think not—and lunch in the Palisades. Then zip to Malibu, which is out there somewhere, and fling ourselves into the ocean, love in the burning sand not being out of the question.

Watch *us!*

As I trace my knowing fingers, as if the very tips have brain cells of their own, along and around each nook and crevice of Dusty Germaine's lithe body as follicle after follicle fairly screams to attention. And my mouth, too, absolutely, tracing every fold and furrow, at the same time holding her down—a neat trick, for she flails out of control. I gently place my hand over her mouth in an act of love, expending only enough pressure to avoid public notice and the police and fire departments, for she wails as an animal yet to be discovered each time I uncover sensations new and sweet and wise, and together we explode, only to begin again, for we are insatiably in love and I am all people and things to her.

Oh, my.

Once in a while I get the itch.

Every day is more like it, I argued back to myself as I lay on my back on my bed, sopping up, trying to hang in there with the knotholes on the ceiling, and not so much as a glance at the telephone.

On the other hand.

I have a hunch that unlike a real school, one has to

know at least a little something about real acting before one just plunks down his ten bucks and starts prancing around yelling Shakespeare.

Or is it enough to act natural?

That is the question.

I didn't expect her to invite me to Rhode Island for Thanksgiving, but I thought possibly we could take in a movie now and then or go for chicken vegetable or up the old Benedict Canyon for a nightcap.

"She outta town, Missa Bwoono! How many time I tow you!" Cato, or whatever the hell his name is.

Mornings I see Miss Dusty the Duster Germaine in a negligee over orange juice and coffee, fingering through *Vogue* while she passes me the toast.

Shall I call her now?

Or wait till tomorrow?

Or just say forget the whole thing?

"Forget the whole thing," says Burt.

"Easy for you to say."

He cocked his head as only he can—believe me I've tried—and regarded me. *"Maybe she really is outta town."* The way he did in *Run Silent, Run Deep,* when Clark Gable went a little apeshit.

"For three months?"

"Four. My guess is she comes and goes." He passed the palms of his hands slowly and quietly by one another. *"Ships in the night."* And smiled that smile.

"I hate to tell you what Jay calls her."

He literally ignored me.

"If you had a name like Scallopine, you'd change it, too." I get a little defensive when I'm tired.

"That's a bridge I never had to cross, kid. Besides, you ain't changed a bit."

I HAVE, TOO, says Jay, so it's debatable. He's looking at my wardrobe, though, I'm sure: my faded sweatshirt, grubby sneakers, and tight jeans. At the mere suggestion of my quandary, he said, "Don't let them change you, baby," so I don't know.

Stan grinned up at me with his lips pressed together, bugged his eyes and poked the side of his head three times with his index finger, as if I was about to discover America.

"WHO AM I?" Phoebe Sax peered down on all twelve of us at the same time, but she stared at me.

The place was a tunnel, except for the four garage doors. It was dank and brown, and leaky, I would imagine, in the wintertime, and cold, and had a little platform that rose about five inches on the far side under the brightest light I ever saw, and rows of squeaky auditorium chairs that faded to black below and beyond. And I was prepared to leave.

"Who . . . am . . . I?" Phoebe Sax repeated in three paragraphs from under the white light. She was thread-like, with frizzy blond hairs all over her head that barely

understood one another, and a voice that roared softly up from her heels. "*That* is the question."

And hot in the summertime I would imagine, when the smell of old wood becomes unbearable.

"And the answer keeps changing!"

Trouble, I thought.

"Agnes de Mille," she concluded, and I was in the dark.

Thankfully, there was a well-lit lobby on the near side with vague tire tracks where the carpet refused to meet and one could presumably take a rest.

I liked the break best.

A sweet fifteen minutes when everybody sort of milled around the lobby of The Little Theatre Off Melrose and smoked and drank coffee and talked, even though I made a fool of myself.

I did not enjoy sitting around on stage, as she called it, in a semicircle, pretending to eat lime ice—"Choose your *absolute* favorite," Phoebe said in a friendly growl— out of a bowl that didn't exist with a spoon that wasn't there, when all there was between my hands and my mouth and my sanity was thin air in the first place. I eat real lime ice five nights a week, overtime on Saturday. And how am I expected to recognize a *real* impulse? I'm a beginner!

"The Brooklyn Dodgers are coming to L.A.!" That's what I chose to announce on the precious break. "It's al- most definite," I added as I sidled up to a face that could easily change a beginner's personality—Claire Something who'd been discussing Somebody Inge. The latest on the National League melted her ice cream, I'm sure.

I should be shot.

Not a beautiful face, but one that could certainly alter the climate of a lobby. "According to the *L.A. Times* sports section," I trailed, scrounging for an ally, nodding pathetically toward Rusty Something, another perfect stranger who happened to be lolling at Claire Whoever's feet along with so many others.

Shot.

"Boy! Boy, I'd like to take her to coffee!" I confessed to the same Rusty later, on the way out of The Little Theatre Off Melrose.

"No, man." He stopped me in my tracks in the middle of the dark sidewalk, put a friendly hand on my shoulder, though we hardly knew one another, and looked up at me, for he was only five-nine. "You'd like to fuck her brains out."

He had a nice quality, so I took Rusty to coffee.

"And I got five bucks says I get there first." Tee-hee-hee, through his back teeth.

"See, Johnny, unlike you . . ." he explained over tea. He'd ordered hot tea ("You know what I'd like, dear? A nice cup of hot tea, dear. Can you do that for me, dear?"). Dear would have put the cash register in the trunk of his VW if he'd asked, and jumped in behind it. "Unlike you, Johnny, I *loved* the army. Hey. Why not? I fucked every nurse, every PX cashier, every WAC that didn't have an ass the size of the Rose Bowl, drank more fuckin' booze, got in more fights, won more bread at liar's poker. You know what I *hated* about the army? The very reason, may God strike me dead, I didn't *stay* in the fuckin' army? Because there was always, I swear to Christ, *always* some dumb motherfucker who couldn't wipe my ass . . ."

"Sergeant Tolliver!" I raised my voice.

". . . tellin' me what the fuck to do!" He raised his voice.

" 'You got aversion to usin' a watch, soldier?' " I couldn't remember the last time I'd raised my voice. " 'Gimme forty and tell me ya love 'em!' " A little louder, why not? " 'I ain't found one thang about you I'd hit a dawg in the ass with . . .' "

"Some mizzable prick standin' on my chest givin' me orders!" Rusty boomed.

Slim Pickens, I decided. " 'What part of shut the fuck up don't you understand?' "

"Who couldn't wipe my ass!"

"Asshole Tolliver!"

"I'm *hip!*"

"You know who you remind me of?" I asked Rusty after the excitement died down.

"Who, champ?"

"James Cagney."

"Oh, *man!*" His eyeballs disappeared into the back of his head. "Old Jimmy? Johnny, that's about the nicest fuckin' compliment you could pay me. Listen," he instructed, leaning over his tea, cupping a hand in secrecy.

"What the fuck you think brought me to Hollywood in the first place?"

"What?" I also leaned.

"Man, he's my *idol!*" He reared back. "I swear to Christ, sometimes Jimmy Cagney almost talks to me."

Rusty Durkin: Boston, south side. We exchanged numbers.

I T ' S *W I L L I A M* I N G E . I looked it up.

"God forbid you should learn something in the process," Stan said to me over the phone.

It's Claire *Fairchild.* Claire Fairchild *Van Horn. Mrs.*

xi
• • •

Call *your agent!* the note said.
I've arrived, my heart giggled as I stood at
the bar in the Raincheck Room. Sardi's West,
we call it. A message, too. Not just a phone call. The
more hands it passes through, the better, I thought, and
I held it for a long time and relished the exclamation
point. I smiled at the ladies to my right and the ladies to
my left.

"What do you feel?" demands Phoebe Sax of us about
three hundred times every Wednesday night. "At this
very second!" she whispers out loud.

In the heart of it, I guess you could say, old Pheeb.

Rusty and I had just taken poor old Frankie Pascuzzi
for twenty-five clams in liar's poker because the dumb
son of a bitch thought a straight beat a full house. The
joint was jumping, is the reason Phil forgot to give me
the note the moment I walked in the door.

"Thanks, Philly, you have no idea what this means to me."

I made my way through the crowd, whistling, of all things, "So long, it's been good ta know ya" between my teeth and when I got back to the booth, Rusty said, "You mean to tell me he didn't hurdle the fuckin' bar the minute you walked in the door?! Man, that's crucial!"

"I told him he had his head up his ass."

"Atta boy, champ."

"SWEETHEART, where've you been?" Ramona talks to me as if she's buttoning my coat for school. "Stanley's been trying to reach you for three days, Sweetheart, hang on."

"Bubbala.* Stan. Where da fuck you been? You by any chance part Hawaiian?"

"Hawaiian?" I exclaimed.

"Yeah."

"Me?"

"Yeah. They wanna see ya for a heavy on *Hotline: Hawaii.* Tomorra, ten o'clock. I sent 'em your pictures. What can I tell ya? They're a little dark, so they thought maybe, and I said sure. Part."

"But I'm not."

"Ya got a tan, am I right?"

"Yeah."

"And you're pushin' twenty-seven, don't lie to me."

"Would I lie?"

*Baby-cakes (nonsexual)

"So you'll go, you'll do, you'll be a how-da-ya-call-it for half an hour. A kanak—ya think I don't know from Hawaiian. Ten o'clock. Write it down."

I SEARCHED all night long, and by nine A.M. I couldn't find Johnny Bruno anywhere. Not in the mirror, not in my head. I couldn't find anybody. Never mind, I had a bell in my heart. Warner Bros., here I come. Building G, Room 232.

It was sunny in Los Angeles.

"Good morning, Mrs. Ward."

"Good morning. Isn't it a lovely day!"

"Bonjour, Finette. Bonjour, Irene!"

"Bonjour, bonjour!"

I drove east on Santa Monica Boulevard past the Arrow, Peter's, Dominic's, and the Raincheck. Whipped left on Harper, a nice class of apartments, right on Fountain, even nicer, and slowed to rich, gray with turrets. Left on Havenhurst, hookers' row, right on Sunset, passed the Garden of Allah, thought of Errol Flynn, crossed Crescent Heights, and waved at the boys at the counter. Up Highland onto the Hollywood Freeway, off at Barham, and was tempted to coast the rest of the way into Burbank, however it was impossible. Parked on Olive. Peace, I thought.

Not every Tom, Dick, and Harry gets inside Warner Bros.

I stated my business in detail to a uniformed guard, an

older gentleman, who issued me a pass and gave me directions as I studied his eyes for secrets. I thanked him more than plenty and shook his hand. He seemed only a little surprised.

I floated through the Main Gate.

"Sweetie, if you don't throw those nice shoulders back I'm just going to give you a good poke," says Ev. "Stand up straight, honey," adds Rose. "It shows confidence."

I hovered among soundstages the size of small towns and the color of fancy mustard, and lost myself in slits of sky and flashing red. "Do not enter."

A group of no-nonsense men wearing hammers guided a mountainside on wheels between me and my destination. They also gave me directions, and moved on. Ships in the night? A woman passed me, younger than I, a cut above, I thought, swinging a portfolio of eleven-by-fourteen glossies. And another and another to and from other directions. I couldn't help stopping, looking back and up and down. Even their legs seemed different from women outside the Main Gate as star of tomorrow after star of tomorrow shoved through space on balled calves.

I treaded thin air and destinations zigzagged.

A smallish man with a load of clothes in his arms and a coat hanger between his teeth rode by on a bicycle and put me straight. Had I seen him before? What movie? I wondered as I drifted toward Building G, and each one I'd ever dreamt flashed before my eyes.

It was a wooden, two-storied bungalow, at least a generation old. How many and whose feet have pushed through this very Building G? I studied the legend in the lobby. How appropriate, I thought. Legend. HOTLINE HAWAII—CASTING. Be still. Second floor. A flight up. Also appropriate. Up, up, up I climbed, taking my sweet hot time, caressing the banister. How many hands, and whose?

I inched toward Room 232.

Opened The Door.

Began to ease in to The Business, as I became aware . . .

How quiet.

Full up, to be sure, but oh so quiet, it came to my attention. To the tune of one woman at a desk, paying little attention, and twelve gnarly Hawaiians hunkering in heaviness.

Real ones from across the blue Pacific.

Not Italian ones from up the coast.

So many mightily flowered shirts hung in such a colorful splash that seemed almost to tent—smother?—the little green reception area. A striking contrast, I observed, my fingers growing damp around the doorknob, to pinstripes from Zeidler and Zeidler. And see those big kanaka fellows pacing and those other big ones slumping. *A Streetcar Named Aloha?*

Interesting, I thought, how they all, to a giant, appear to be brooding, a brown study if you will, a tooth-grinding, knuckle-cracking, wall-clawing, dead-quiet frenzy that chewed up the room and ate it.

I closed the door so soundlessly I could hear the little

bell in my heart grow faint, stop dead, and fall to the base of my nuts.

"Name?" she asked, glancing up from the carpet of glossies that covered her desk.

"Hmmm?" I inquired pleasantly.

She poised a wet nail brush with aplomb in one hand, hung the other helplessly out to dry. Grace Kelly, probably, except for the gum.

"Name?"

That I heard myself respond "Bruno Sangenito" in an octave reeking of popcorn and licorice sticks was fortunate in a sense, for the adult quickly reached down and slapped the bejeesus out of the child. The kid slapped back and, as a couple grappling, they collapsed into a coughing jamboree which nearly felled Building G, Room 232 and temporarily reinstated my genitals. Screw the bell.

"Johnny Bruno!" I pounced.

Creative recovery, I thought.

"Join the club," she said.

What will they want of me? I wondered as I joined the others. To sing a song, tell a joke? When are my eyes intense and when are they not? I don't know any jokes, I thought as I dried and redried my palms on my pants and gave myself a hell of a manicure with my incisors. How do I act in the Inner Office? I asked myself. One by one, kanak after kanak trod through yet another Door within the Room inside the Building within the Gate that Jack built. I have *what* is it again, and don't know it?

What will they want and how will I make it happen?
Which Hat? Pin the tail on the quality. It *is* a club, I
thought.

I'm going home.

Goodbye My Fancy, So Goes My Love, and *Sayonara.*

1. Call Rusty.

2. Call Stan.

Because I have no business in *this* business, like no
business I know. I'll rejoin the army and go to officers' . . . Shut up, I said to myself, you typist. Face it,
you're an usherette.

3. Call Jay.

4. Call Walt.

Clean your own surps.

You turd, I said to myself—and I never say that word
because I can't stand the sound of it.

You turd!

5. Call Ev.

"Sweetie, get off the toilet, you'll get piles like
Charles—the size of buffalo nickels, Dr. Quisenberry
says."

I care not.

Give me hemorrhoids or give me death.

Leg of lamb and crispy potatoes, here I come.

6. Call Phoebe.

She won't care. She'll be happy. Good riddance, she'll
think.

WASSA MATTA you is hardly the most difficult chunk of dialog to utter convincingly. Wassa matta you wassa matta you wassa matta you—that wasn't so hard now, was it? One can easily utter it with significance sitting on the john or slouching in a blue suit at the luau, as it were, offering eye avoidance and slippery handshakes to the producer and director of *Hotline: Hawaii*—who own my future.

Wassa matta *me*, I thought.

"Wassa matta *you!*" I growled at the top of something with my toes all scrunched, as if I were kicking myself.

"MAZEL TOV," said Stan.

xii

• • •

Bing Crosby crooned, "You Belong to My Heart." M-7 on the best jukebox in town.

"You don't have to show that to your wife or anything." Margie chuckled, indicating my tasteful leather purse, in which I had carefully placed her snapshot next to my extravagant Dunhill, both of which were gifts from Claire.

Show me a man with a purse, the card had read, and I'll show you a man who looks good in his jeans.

"Moi?" I exaggerated.

"She'd never understand, and I wouldn't blame her," she added, hoarsely. "Hah."

"No wife."

"No?"

"Uh-uh."

"You're kidding."

"How's your drink?" I probed, in search of the perfect transition.

"After all these years?"

"I have hair transplants."

"Huh?"

"Right here. See?"

"I don't get it."

"I wouldn't be caught dead in a toupee."

"You mean instead?"

"Of what?"

"A wife."

"No. You said after all these years, and I could've sworn you were looking at my head. See? Right up here. See?"

"Ouch. Did it hurt?"

"Not much."

"Were you *ever* married?"

"No, you're looking in the wrong place. The light's bad. See these little haystacks? Where my finger's pointing!"

"I bet you had an opportunity or two or three."

"Actually, it's not totally painless. They do stick novocaine into your skull."

"Ouch."

"About a hundred times. Mostly it's the bleeding."

"The bleeding?"

"They try to hide it, but it's there."

"I can't stand the sight of blood."

"It's there. Sometimes you can feel it. And the noise."

"Noise?"

"Yeah, they gouge out—"

"*Wow*, it's getting crowded in here!" Margie shuddered, stretching a giant stretch, arms extended, fists clenched, scanning the scene.

"Sleepy?"

"Hell, no."

"Like coring an apple."

"How's *yours?*" she asked, coming down all ashudder, focusing on nothing.

"What?"

"Drink."

"Jim-dandy." I smiled.

". . . ."

". . . ." And continued to do so.

"Gee!"

"What?"

"It must be more goddamn fun being in the movies!"

"Heathcliff, can you see the gray over there where our castle is?"

Wuthering Heights
UNITED ARTISTS, 1939

"Your left eye says yes, and your right eye says no. Fifi, you're cockeyed!"

The Merry Widow
MGM, 1934

xiii
• • •

Possibly it was my tan. Thankfully, I maintain a deep tan. Although that doesn't make sense under the circumstances. Maybe the fact that it's a light tan. By comparison. The suit. I believe the suit helped rather than hindered, although one would think . . .

Don't ask! Awright awreddy, it's a freaky business. Thank you, Stan, for launching my career. Next, ladies and gentlemen, I'd like to thank an aging priest in a little parish in a small . . . Obviously, it was the way I delivered the line. How did I do that? I did not smile, I definitely recall not smiling. Ev, may I present Mrs. Ward? How lovely of you to have us all, Jane. I believe you know my fantasy, Claire—Jay, say hello to Rusty, Rusty, say hello to Jay. No. It was the handshake. People love a firm sincere handshake of some duration. And unless I miss my guess, Hawaiians are by nature non-talkative.

On the other hand.

Have I got something?

"Or have I got something!?" I hollered at the ceiling as I lay on my back on my bed, blithely bouncing.

Buck Jones blew smoke from the muzzle of his frontier .45 and holstered same. Mary, who had been protected all the while under Buck's other arm, breathed a sigh of relief and gave him a big kiss on the cheek. He couldn't handle it, she'll teach him.

As time went by, Richard Blaine, better known as Rick, reunited with Ilsa by sheer accident on top of the Empire State Building.

The statuesque blonde burst into my office without knocking. She was uptown. Real uptown. I hadn't paid my rent in three months, and she looked as if she had her foot on a hundred dollar bill.

FADE IN:

EXT. DOCK—DAY

THUG #1 (menacing, mid-forties) and THUG #2 (menacing, mid-twenties) lurk in the shadows. They crouch, watching, listening from behind precarious stack of barrels containing contraband. We SEE inconspicuous SEDAN in the b.g. CAMERA PANS to include LANCE and LORRAINE as they approach.

                    LANCE
          We have reason to believe that Lattimer was in-
          volved in your father's death.

> LORRAINE
> (shaken)

Uncle Junius?

> LANCE
> (comforting)

I'm afraid so.

> LORRAINE
> (disbelief)

That's impossible!

> LANCE

He stands to inherit millions.

> LORRAINE

But the orphanage! Daddy's will specifically
states—

> LANCE
> (interrupting)

Depends on which will you're reading, Miss
Ridgeway.

> LORRAINE
> (stunned)

You mean . . . ?

> LANCE

Shall we discuss it over dinner?

At which point our thugs emerge from hiding. Thug #1
rabbit-punches Lance from behind. Stunned, he falls to his
knees, recovers in time to see . . .

Lance's POV. Thug #2 forces Lorraine into sedan, meantime Thug #1 bolts to the driver's side, Thug #2 at-
tempting to jump into the now moving vehicle.

Lance dives, catches Thug #2 by the ankles as car speeds
off. Thug #2 recovers and moves toward Lance.

THUG #2
(menacingly)
Wassa matta you?!

Thug #2 swings a haymaker to the jaw, catching Lance off guard. Lance shakes off the punch and crumples #2 with a crushing right to the ribs, sending him sprawling into the barrels, which come tumbling down on his soon-to-be-lifeless body.

WE HEAR SIRENS.

FADE OUT.

It was fine.

Cut, print, they said.

Malibu is lovely this time of year, and it's amazing how much it probably looks exactly like Hawaii. *Location*, it's called. I said the word aloud, and took note of everything under the sun as I drove home from the *shoot* along Pacific Coast Highway, which is devastatingly gorgeous at sunset. After we *wrapped*. Finished.

Just fine.

Jock Jason was born to play Lance. Apparently. What a neat guy. Imagine breaking bricks with the heel of one's hand between takes. Imagine a TV star with a reputation for single-handedly cleaning out bars in the valley, yet being notoriously cordial on the set.

Nobody's perfect.

Sharon Briscoe is perfect. Also formidable, and friendly, too, I would imagine under normal circumstances, although one can hardly expect Lorraine to chat it up with every thug in the company.

I did not hurt her hair on purpose.

It's going to be fine.

Fascinating, how she kept asking Jock to show her his gun. Cute little gun. She practically licked his face. It was fun to watch. I can't believe it takes Makeup half an hour to regulate his shitty little curl.

I never threw a girl into a car before, is all. I think Hair understood that fact. It wasn't an enormous delay, nor was the bump on her arm for that matter, even though we were losing our light, and the director shook his head and looked at the sky again and muttered *son of a bitch*. I liked him, too.

The homes, I notice, along Pacific Coast Highway face the ocean. I wonder which is considered front and which is considered back. What difference does it make?

Left on Sunset Boulevard. If I turn right, I drive directly into the black Pacific.

Not to worry. Marie Rosario drifted by. There's a first time for everything.

The crew, to a man, knew it was an accident. Ice for Jocko's jaw! One would think he was Laurence Olivier.

"Depends on which rill you're weeding, Miss Widgeray." Twenty minutes. I'd like to have a kwack at that one.

Instead of a lucky guy in a tight T-shirt, which is what he is.

Ice for Jocko's jaw! He's very handsome.

How 'bout a little for Sangenito's rib?

And gracious and muscular.

Hello there, Pacific Palisades. Brentwood and Beverly Hills coming up on the opposite horizon. And step on it.

And take it from the top, why don't you, you clumsy jackass?

Why the gun? Why a gun in a person's belt in the first place at the last possible minute? Their mistake. Props. Not mine.

Quiet on the set!

Where is it written, as Stan would say, that Thug #2 is supposed to have a weapon the size of Waikiki? That wasn't even remotely suggested in the script. And stuck into his baggy trousers at the last possible second!

For safety.

But it's trickling.

Action!

Down the seersucker.

We'll never see it.

Yeah, but nip, nip, nip.

Out of frame, they said. Action for chrissake, they added.

Understandably.

Emerge, shove (sorry), run, jump, dive, fall . . .

"Wassa matta *you*?"

Or did I say, "Wassa *matta* you!"

What possible difference?

Socko, Jocko, that's the point!

Not to mention Jocko, socko back.

Now just calm down. Just. Calm. Down. What did we learn today?

1. Less is more.

2. One does not need to miss *close* when one throws a punch?

3. The lens distorts. I'll buy that crazy dream.

Shall I punch this oncoming truck? Or just miss close?

The fall, they liked. I'm sure they did. I think I heard them say as much during my apologies. Cast and crew to a man to a woman loved the tackle and the fall. It *worked*, they said. My director's name is Charlie ("Call me Charlie"). We'll do it again one day.

The nurse was Rosalind Russell. "Leave the bandages on those knees till morning," she advised, not without humor, and I was either Fred MacMurray or Alexander Knox. I couldn't remember which.

If I'm not mistaken, I think I put the accent on the *wassa*.

xiv
• • •

"**S**hake out your wrists!" little Phoebe the Lion-hearted strongly suggested. She paced the aisle in giant strides, yet paid extreme attention to the solitary figure under the light. "Harder!" she added in that muffled echo-ridden baritone that can scare the crap out of you if it's your turn in the barrel. "Now let them *drop* to your sides of their own accord. Exactly! Feeeel the tingle?"

The solitary figure began to form an answer.

"No words!" commanded Phoebe.

Not easy for Claire Fairchild Van Horn, who loves to rant on. She's terribly intellectual—intellectual*ized*, Phoebe says. I don't think there was anyone in the rest of the litter who thought it was a real question.

"Now stretch your arms toward the ceiling as if you could almost touch it."

Jesus, Van Horn has long arms, I thought.

"Now, merely *allow* them to flop to your sides."

Legs, too.

"Allow your chin to *drop* to your chest."

No chest, however.

"Feeeel your jaw . . ."

Strong.

". . . go slack. Your mouth . . ."

Wide.

". . . your cheeks."

Narrow.

One could almost hear an ego drop, as Phoebe is fond of insisting. She refuses to have it any other way. That's how quiet it was in The Little Theatre Off Melrose. I'm not sure whether Claire looks better with the glasses—too hip for words—or without. If one observes from the front row, one can't help noticing the little hole, barely big enough to place the tip of a swizzle stick, that forms in the absolute center of her mouth when she's totally at peace. She's a bit of a know-it-all, is the fact of the matter.

"Take a deeeep breath," directed Phoebe. "Exhale slowly. Allow a sound. Don't *make* a sound. *Allow* a sound, not a noise, a *sound* . . .

"Allow . . .

"A sound . . .

"To *happen!*" she chanted out of some uncharted jungle.

Sometimes in class I don't know who the hell to look at.

"Uuuuuuhhggg . . ." growled Miss Park Avenue, right

at me, I could have sworn, out of some skinny part of her hipless pelvis—as if to say: pay attention, you horse's ass.

Phoebe crept upright onto the stage and placed a straight-backed chair behind Claire's sagging pointy knees, encased obviously in the baggiest jeans she could find, and eased her into it. She picked up Claire's muckalucks one at a time by the toe and let each long foot drop to the floor, bang. Took her gently by the middle finger of each hand, lifted and rubberized each arm and let fall. Hardly the most conservative wedding ring on the planet. Phoebe teaches us to be observant. Also to keep it simple.

"Be aware that your ring finger is indicating." Meaning wiggling, telling a story. "And stop it this instant." Lovingly said.

And she did.

"Choose a place to *be*, one in which you've been, a risky place, and create just that atmosphere . . .

"*Hear* the sounds . . .

"*Smell* the smells, get wet with it . . .

"*Visualize* shapes and colors and sizes. Notice, my darlings, how the body begins slowly to change of its own accord . . ."

And it did.

". . . when one deals in the sensory."

As it took an eon, it seemed, for her legs to draw up of their own accord and shorten, and longer even for her knees to come together as a child's on the potty, and the remainder of her to slouch, and her elbows to seek eventual unrest on top of each thigh. Claire cupped her face in her hands, clenched her fingers, stared at space and hid nothing.

"Let the tears come," concluded Phoebe.

Somebody guessed that she was visiting a dying friend in the hospital. Some other idiot guessed she was putting her Labrador to sleep. I guessed she was reading a very sad book in a large metropolitan library, but kept my big mouth shut.

She simultaneously wiped her eyes with the sleeve of her bulky very faded gray sweatshirt which came down to the upper part of her long slender fingers which had fuzz, and laughed out loud.

"Sitting on the john in a Monterey Park motel," she admitted.

I, for one, was surprised.

" Do you take cream?" I asked.

"Black," Claire replied.

"Me, too. Sugar?"

"Never."

"Great minds . . ." I started, and staggered off into a great abyss.

I wouldn't even be close to the edge, I thought, if I hadn't stopped in the lobby to congratulate her on her commitment to the sensory, then launched into a glorious account of my vast television experience, cast and crew, and Phoebe hadn't capped off the evening with a fairly intriguing lecture on impulse. "*Never* ignore a first impulse," she'd said. "It comes like a breath of fresh wind," she breathed. "And is gone." If Claire hadn't left the lights on in her fancy Pontiac and I hadn't produced the jumper cables from my grubby trunk, I wouldn't even be teetering.

"You don't like me very much, do you," she said. It was hardly a question.

"No. I mean, I *do*."

"Ha, ha," she said with a mouthful of pie, not particularly trying to hide it.

"No. I do."

"Frankly, I haven't been too crazy about you, either."

"I knew it."

"Yeah, but you knew it before I decided it. I almost fell into my fan belt when you asked me to have coffee. Where's your friend, Rusty?"

"He quit. He thinks Phoebe's full of shit."

"He's an asshole."

"Actually, we're very close."

"How 'bout them Dodgers."

"So . . . what's your husband's name, anyway?"

"Lucky."

"Lucky Van Horn?"

"Lucky Van Horn."

"So . . . nearsighted or farsighted?"

"Astigmatism."

"Really?"

"Yeah."

"Me, too."

"Really?"

"I think. A little."

"You'll probably need glasses . . ."

"Should have 'em now probably."

". . . someday."

"I ought to check that out."

"You really should."

"Tomorrow, probably. So . . . anyway, I had this dream about you the other night," I confessed. "I actually did."

"Well?"

"Yeah. As it turned out, we were floating in this swimming pool, you and me—or is it you and I? I never know . . ."

"I."

"How's your pie?"

"Good. Yours?"

"Good. And we had suits of armor on."

"Subtle. Want a bite?"

"Sure, you want a bite?"

"Sure."

Claire put a little lemon meringue on my plate and I put a little French apple on hers.

Dupar's, Farmers Market, Third and Fairfax: September 22, 1960.

AWARENESS is *everything*. Phoebe's Law. I'm not clear on that yet. You could fill a book with my gray area. But

I was prepared to give it some thought as I drove and the scabs on my knees played a happy tune, which hardly makes sense, on the inside of my jeans and yanked at me every time I lifted my foot to apply the brake. I finally found a parking place way the hell up Sweetzer and decided to sit for a while and force myself to reflect on my new career.

Who does she remind me of?

I've never known a Claire before.

"I like your hair," I'd admitted, shortly after she'd refused a second refill. "A little bit like Ingrid Bergman in—"

"*For Whom the Bell Tolls?*"

"Yeah."

"After the fascist bastards shaped it into a devastatingly attractive bob?"

"Yeah."

"What a lovely thing to say."

She doesn't remind me of anybody. She reminds me of a nut.

"Long story boring," she explained, choosing not to. "I've got to get my ass home. We're off to New York at the crack."

A nut who crumples at accidental humor, and staggers unselfconsciously the width of the parking lot, and leans back like a silly crane against the door of her attractive blue Bonneville, and looks a fellow straight in the eye and shakes his hand.

A month is a long time, I thought, as she further explained. "Possibly two," even longer. "Night, Johnny B., we'll do it again."

A smart-assed, lighthearted, married nut.

The Crimson Pirate swooped immediately and acrobatically onto my passenger seat and held me at sword's point. *"None of my business, kid."* But one was aware he was making it so. *"None of my business."*

"Who asked you, Burt? Did you hear me crying out in the goddamn wilderness all of a sudden?"

"It's your affair."

"Who said anything about an affair? Did I mention affair? Even once? I'm trying to reflect on my burgeoning career, if you were paying attention."

"Depends on how bad you need it, kid."

I tightened my eyes and did something familiar with my jaw. *"Depends on how bad you need it, kid."* I must say I do a mighty fine impression.

Naturally, he answered with that insightful smile.

She's a leading lady is what she is. Part of her anyway. "When I was little," she'd confided on our way to the cash register, "I didn't know whether I wanted to grow up to be Katharine Hepburn or Eleanor Roosevelt." A leading lady in disguise.

It was exactly two hundred and twelve steps from my birdshit-laden fender-bendered, tar-stained '51 Chevy that reeks of burnt ignition wire, speaking of the sensory, to the front door of the Raincheck Room.

"You're late, man!" yelled Rusty, banging his fist in mock indignation as I moved toward the booth.

"Car trouble," I said.

"You're also buying, motherfucker, since you're a big television star. Quick," he added slyly, "here comes Pascuzzi. Get your dollar bills out."

"Tell me again. A straight beats a full house, right?"

I wonder if part of her needs a leading man.

"The other way around, champ."

XV
• • •

I'm aware that I'd rather take the train.

I'm almost aware that I'd rather spend Christmas making double time making double scoops than watch Ev and Aunt Rose duke it out over who taught who to get the potatoes so crispy. If I make it home at all. Having witnessed the "Dockside Danger" episode of *Hotline: Hawaii*—aired nationwide—I'm fully aware I photograph like a gargoyle, hadn't nearly enough screen time, and deserve to be dead. And every time an air pocket has its way with us, I'm more than aware I haven't a bubble of talent. Yet, please God, don't let me go before my next picture. Furthermore, I'm convinced that if I stick the plug of my Sunbeam Shavemaster into the little holes provided in the john, PSA Flight 1117 will go down in sparks over the Santa Cruz Mountains.

STAR FOUND IN TAIL,

RAZOR EMBEDDED . . .

I weighed the importance of looking sensational when one deplanes.

" N OW TELL ME , what's that all about?"

"What's that, Aunt Rose?"

"The haircut."

"It's a Sebring cut."

"That don't mean anything to me," said Rose, erasing the air between us with a wig-wag of her world-famous stuffed celery (Philadelphia cream cheese, green onions, a dot of mustard), indicating that if it don't mean a whole lot to her, it don't mean a whole lot.

"It's a *style*," explained Ev from the kitchen. "Sweetie, tell Aunt Rose about your part."

"It's on the left."

"And what fun it was."

"Well," I began, "Long story boring . . ."

"Honey, if it's boring, spare me," said Aunt Rose.

"No, no," I explained. "Merely a figure of speech."

"I don't think it's boring at all!"

"I know, Mom. I don't, either. It's just a figure of speech."

"It's a *new* figure of speech!" enthused Ev, nodding toward Rose on reentry into the dining room. "Isn't it, sweetie?"

"So tell us!" ordered Rose, stalk at half-staff. "And honey," she instructed parenthetically but not unpleasantly toward Evelyn, now seated at attention, "my celery

don't *need* this crap [paprika] all over it. It's called gild-
ing the lily. So bore us."

Where to begin, I wondered, and just how much of my
on-camera life do I feel comfortable sharing? I snap-
decided to relate a brief version of the heroics I'd spun
for Ev over a drink under the tree the night before
Christmas. Cut and print, I explained: they loved what
they loved what they loved—which seemed sufficient, for
I was aware that floor time at the dinner table with *The
Dolly Sisters* was precious—and that in all probability
yours truly and Sharon Briscoe would be seen lunching
at the Polo Lounge in the very near—

"She's a Gemini, that one . . ."

"Bullshit! That's all I have to say on that subject."

". . . if you can believe what you read nowadays."

My mother admitted sure enough there I was big as
life on the TV, and my aunt confessed to being on the
toilet at the time.

We all agreed momentarily that Ev's gelatin salad was
the best ever, "wooster" sauce being not the least of a
host of sacred ingredients from the mouth of Charles
Newman's maiden sister's kitchen in far off Santa Rosa,
where he was presumably enjoying the holiday. Aunt
Rose later confided to me from behind a turkey leg that
she never could understand gelatin salad in the first
place, and she thought Ev whipped it up every year just
to get her goat.

"And honey, it's wis-ter-shere, not wooster. Ye gods . . ."

"Charles says wooster."

"Ye gods . . ."

Ev chuckled and passed me a dish of Rose's world famous cranberry sauce (four to two to one, cranberries to sugar to water) and kept chuckling, "What I want to know and so does your Aunt Rose is what in the world you're going to do with the rest of your life *now*." And kept chuckling. "Isn't that right, Aunt Rose?"

"And honey, loosen those jeans for God's sake." Rose chuckled. "I never saw such tight jeans in my life. This white meat is *so* juicy—that's how you can tell if it's a good turkey, if the white meat is juicy. I don't think Peter wears them that tight. Where'd you get such a good turkey, Evelyn, I want to know right this instant!"

"Safeway."

"Will wonders never cease."

"How's Peter?" I asked, referring to a cousin I hadn't seen since days of Santa Cruz and Let's Pretend.

"My little boy, Peter?" Rose lifted both knife and fork and poised them vertically as if to call for quiet on the set. "He's down *there*, don'tcha know." And waved them back and forth at odds with one another, indicating nowhere.

"Where?"

"Hollywood."

"No."

"*Yes*, being a writer. Think about that, honey. You should finish college . . ."

Shirley Temple pursed her lips and passed the yams (hers, marshmallow). "Aunt Rose and I were talking about college *just* the other night . . ."

". . . Honey, that's where it all starts, with the writer. I never understood marshmallows . . ."

". . . weren't we, Aunt Rose?"

"Think about it for a minute and remind me to give you his number."

"Me kennit zitzen mit ein tuchus aft svey irriden."

". . . ."

". . . ."

"That sounds very fancy to say the least, and pray tell what is my stuffing [Rose's W.F. Italian] doing all by its lonesome over there?"

"You can't put one ass on two seats at the same time," I translated, passing the stuffing.

"In what language, pray tell?"

"Jewish."

Ev retreated to the kitchen and returned in silence with a larger spoon for the stuffing, Rose struggled endlessly with gristle, and I helped myself to seconds on everything.

I BECAME AWARE as our sleek 707 made a flawless approach through the murky southern California skies toward the big runway, how small Granville had grown over time. I'd become aware of many things during my solo tour earlier in the day. *Ben Hur* was playing at the little El Rey. Imagine Stephen Boyd. I wanted to gag. Attractive, sure, but a stick at any price: I doffed my sunglasses for more than a split second and saw myself large in a chariot. The Cosgrove house on Baywood was newly painted green, with darker green trim that rendered it even smaller. Dark colors do that, it's good to reflect. The cement path was still a cement path, as was the shrubbery shrubbery. I wondered where they were as I became aware that the pungent eucalyptus never changes, and marveled at how little we all had in common. *"Are you also aware, kid, that you're becoming a slight pain in the ass?"* I heard a smile murmur, then quickly perished the thought as we touched down safely in Burbank, not far from Warner Bros.

xvi
• • •

I plucked at the perimeter of my soppy cocktail napkin in order to create a perfect circle under my
glass, and Margie sucked ice.

I took little notice of my watch.

It was elevenish.

"You know what?" she asked.

Time to shake this dive, is what, finish our circle and
call it a night. "What?"

"How come you never called?"

Hug my pillow, put my banky on nine. "When?" Knowing full well.

"After we broke up."

Or glaze my eyes and clutch my heart and sink to the
floor, imagine sirens, visualize paramedics, possibly break
my jaw on the lip of the table . . .

"Sentimental Journey" was playing on the jukebox.
Doris Day.

Rocky road.

An impulse whipped at me like a breath of fresh Scotch.

"Well," I spun, "I just figured a flower lei will either float in or float out, when you consider the vastness of the ocean and that we experience only the top of it, depending on where it's meant to float . . ."

"I have to go potty."

"Of course. All the way back and to your right, best knock."

"Small, huh?"

"Unisex." She'll never understand.

"Huh?"

"Like home."

"You're kidding."

"Would I kid?"

"You used to tell the best jokes," she said, scootching. "You used to tickle the hell out of me." Scootch, scootch. "What the hell," she added, unraveling, "maybe I'll just bust right in and get lucky, hah! No, just kidding."

I watched her go.

Been done, I thought, and scootched in place.

And watched her little loose-fitting black pants suit grow smaller and smaller, as if the big camera had pulled all the way back from foggy Tuesday and misty windshield—a squint if one thinks through the proper lens— till it was clear she was destined to become a dot on the screen, and I pondered the double-dimpled ass as a category.

When out jumped a fawn.

Out of the jungle and jangle of bottles and bangles and glasses and glitter . . .

Appeared . . .

Emmis . . .

The original of the category: fawn.

My booth runneth over.

And the creature stood and arched a little, alone of a summer's evening, it appeared.

A wake-up call in a mink to remember, wearing an elegant slip of a something underneath.

"Behold!" said Nikki Gentry. "A face from your wicked wicked past." *Pahst* in fawn language.

I stood.

We clasped.

A passerby half her age tarried to admire, which startled the fawn. She regarded him with a thread of disdain that used to make my dick hard, then brightened. "We were starlets together," she explained to the passerby.

"We all have our daydreams. Mine has just gone
a step further than most people's."

Separate Tables
UNITED ARTISTS, 1958

". . . you've moved bag and baggage into your
own fantasy world."

Who's Afraid of Virginia Woolf?
WARNER BROS., 1966

xvii

• • •

They bulldozed The Garden of Allah. Rumor has it Litton Savings is coming to the corner of Sunset and Havenhurst. And guess who made confetti out of Dusty the Duster's phone number and let it go little by little out the window on the Hollywood Freeway.

I feel a change coming on.

Jay and I make it a point to have a little bite together—din-din, he calls it—every Thursday night at Musso's, except for the week I spent in a water tank in Glendale being Lobster Man in *Trouble at the Seashore*. Cheer up, Stan says, nobody will ever see dis picture. "Din-din?" I asked Jay when he first suggested it over herb tea. *"Din-din?"* I think I raised my eyebrows, and so what if I did. "You *must* be joking." When in Rome.

A surge of savvy.

Once in a while I catch a glimpse of Ritchie the Rembrandt in Schwab's and I forsake my soup and swing to the far end of the store—"*Hi*, Bruno Sangenito/Johnny Bruno!"—swoop through perfumes, between notions, veer right at prescriptions, duck into a vacant booth, and pretend Tarzan on phone with Jane.

I don't see this as a contradiction.

I feel . . . not an acceptance, necessarily . . .

Three fan letters poured in. Father Tiv recognized me even with the harpoon through my claw. Ev and Rose each sent along a natural bristle hairbrush with instructions to brush *up* for goodness sakes and *into* the bathroom sink. And one postcard: Gstaad is divine this time of year, according to the Lucky Van Horns. I'll look it up.

But a realization that at six P.M. on any given day my life could change dramatically.

My photo appears on page 134 of the *Academy Players Directory,* a copy of which sits in every casting office in the known world, under the category "Leading Men." My apartment at The Clifford, corner Hayworth and Fountain, has a pool.

Anything is possible.

I voted for John F. Kennedy and would very much like to take the Mrs. to coffee.

Long story boring, I love this town.

On those occasions when I feel a strain on the relationship, I console myself with the fact that if every actor in the community quit his part-time job, no one would get his hat or his oil checked, his milk delivered, house painted, pool cleaned, dinner served, or hair set, and Hollywood would sink to its knees.

"GUESS WHAT, MAN," said Rusty Durkin, leaning over my long gray metal file drawer, one hand on my back, the other cupped around his mouth, fingers atwitch, indicating the utmost confidentiality.

I placed my index finger between the B's and the C's and looked up. "What?"

Rusty has what is known as a nasal stop, according to Phoebe, which, as she explained on his last night in class, is not an impediment exactly, but a way of swallowing one's L's after certain consonants so they come out of one's mouth sounding like soft G's.

"I just got bgowed."

"No!"

He executed a little Irish jig between my bank of files, A through M, and his, N through Z. "I swear to Christ."

"When?"

"On the coffee break." Tee-hee-hee, through his back teeth.

"No!"

A little Art Carney shuffle, to the clackety-clack of various calculators the size of VWs that suck up file cards 'round the clock and belch them out with little rectangular holes all over them, meaning something or other. "The old redhead strikes again!"

"Who?"

I scanned the area. JoAnn, pencil in mouth, typed

nearby, as did Pam and Pat and Paula. Charlene eased between us with a basket of J's and K's.

He tweaked an imaginary bow tie. "Bobbi Jean Whipple."

"No!"

Without question the sexiest keypunch operator on the entire data process floor, swing shift, Hilton Carte Blanche Credit Card Corporation, whose husband works days so nobody had ever met him, much less knew him.

"As God is my judge." Up shot Rusty's right hand, left hand solemnly over his heart area, head hung in humility.

Only the other night the two musketeers had plotted successfully to summon the same Bobbi Jean away from her machine to the telephone on a remote desk fifty feet away just to watch her whipple the distance. "You *guys!*" she'd said, shaking her pretty little head at the carpet as she whippled slowly back across the miles to keypunch.

"Where?"

"Men's room."

"No!"

"Third stall."

"*No!*"

Yes.

Apparently.

I SLUMPED over my Schlitz and studied the rim of my glass. We sat, backs to the front door at the near corner of the bar. I don't think it was very busy. It doesn't matter. Rusty's left hand lay easy around the base of his bottle. With a strong right he clutched his glass. I had just returned from the men's, which at the Raincheck is dim enough so that the image off the mirror is not totally unappealing. I think they use a forty-watt bulb.

I'd come to a conclusion.

Rusty disagreed.

"It's not that you don't have the hang of it, champ. It's that you're too nice."

"You think?"

"Hey, man, would your old dad lie to you?"

"Too nice, huh?"

"Pgease." He raised a hand in mild protest. "Don't get me wrong, Johnny, nice is what I like about you . . . no, man, nice is what I fuckin' love about you. A nicer guy never walked the face of the fuckin' earth. But take tonight for instance."

"Tonight?"

"Tonight, when the new guy came up to you at the drinking fountain and asked you where the pencil sharpener was . . ."

"Yeah?"

"You actually brushed a piece of lint off his jacket. I swear to Christ, I wanted to slap your fuckin' hand away.

You don't pick fuckin' lint off *nobody*, man! To make a long story short, you gotta be a Bogarter in this life, you wanna score."

"A Bogarter, you're right."

"Goddamn right I'm right. Can you see in your wildest fuckin' dreams Bogart wipin' a piece 'a lint off some faggot cocksucker's jacket? Tell him to shove his pencils up his ass. Hey, Philly!" Rusty yelled, stretching most of his five-foot-nine-inch frame off his stool and above the bar. "You mizzable prick, it's about time the house bought a drink!"

"You're probably right."

I HAD just returned from the men's. The journey from booth four to the far end of the room on the chic side of Musso's is flanked by a gauntlet of twelve booths, six on the left and six on the right. Counting passage to and from equals twenty-four possibilities, and eye contact is vital.

"You're wrong, baby."

"I don't think so. Shall we have the broiled chicken?"

Musso's has more tempting suggestions.

"Personally, I'm leaning toward the chiffonade," said Jay, sipping his daiquiri. "You're ballsy enough, God knows. Just look around you."

The booths are bloodred, framed in dark oak, and most of the waiters are Bogarters.

"Maybe a big thick juicy steak."

"Why do you imagine Montgomery Clift is such a raging success for heaven's sake?"

"Yeah, Montgomery Clift."

"It's your sweetness that's going to make it happen for you, baby, and I say if it fits, pick it up and wear it."

"Montgomery Clift. I never thought of that."

"Or the rarebit. Remember we had it the first night?"

THE FAMOUS Phoebe Sax says man is a unit of infinite possibilities. A latent everything. I wonder about that.

MARILYN MONROE would be my first choice as a constant companion. As long as I'm dreaming, Debbie Reynolds would be my second. Having either star's famous arm entwined in one's own—or for that matter being seen nose to nose soda-sipping with Sandra Dee, my third—would be tantamount to playing the second lead in a movie, the importance of which drops rung by rung depending on how far one is required to step down the dream ladder. Imagine the premieres.

I saw Nikki Gentry's panties before I saw her face, which is unusual.

The reason I prefer the Laundromat located exactly forty-seven paces west of the Daisy Fresh is that it reminds me of the good old days, and I make it a point to have egg salad—bonjour, bonjour—during rinse.

Red, black, white, pink, tiny bundles of puffy elegance

scattered helter-skelter over the top of the long Formica table. Beige, lavender even, which piqued me, all perky and hot out of the dryer. *Spin* had spun, and I dug at my sweatshirts, pretending not to notice. Presently, I checked my hair in the window of my own little dryer, put a nickel into the slot, and I think I turned around nice as you please, but I can't be sure.

She wore red heels and shorts that bit at her. I recognized her from *Photoplay*.

"Excuse me," I said, "but don't you find that the dryer really raises Cain with the elastic on stuff, like the stuff you have here on the table. I mean assuming it's yours. It's probably not even yours. I'm sorry, but it's just that I've always heard . . ."

She whipped.

Her lithe body arched, her considerable calves tightened, her lean thighs shimmered in a ray of sunlight that was certainly not around in the good old days, but these were new days. Her face, a perfect heart, was softly framed in beige silk, a scarf among scarves which all but hid her giant rollers, and she had a quality.

Freeze frame.

A tiny lavender pair dangled midair and helplessly between angular thumb and angular forefinger. Obviously I had startled her mid-fold. Her remaining eight fingers stayed splayed, motionless, alert . . .

Her innocent eyes widened and she looked at me as if I had thrown up on her bath towels.

"I beg your pardon?"

"If I'm not mistaken, and I sure could be dead wrong, my understanding is that heat from the dryer really raises Cain with delicate stuff. Probably not."

"*Oh?*"

British.

"You know, like they don't last as long . . ."

"*Oh?*"

Definitely British.

"Yeah, the elastic—"

"Are you a laundry expert?"

"Who, me? No, not at all—far from it. But my mother always says—"

"Aren't you a little old to be living with your mother?"

"Who, me? No, not at all—far from it. She sends them in the mail. You know . . . helpful hints?"

"You're very sweet."

If I know Montgomery Clift, he would most certainly offer to help the famous Nikki Gentry fold her sheets, which were flowered and pink and no trouble at all, and offer to carry her clean warm things to the car, probably a Jag.

"I don't drive."

"Really?"

"Yes, *really*." She reprimanded me, then looked for a moment as if she were going to run and hide. "Not everyone drives, you know. Usually I get picked up. I have a lot of friends."

"Are you getting picked up now?"

"That's very funny. No, I walked. Walking's very healthy, you know, but I am rather tired."

Her apartment had high ceilings, hardwood floors, and white nubbly genuine lath-and-plaster walls, the kind you normally can't drive a nail through.

Everybody was there. Bob Hope, Frank Sinatra, John Wayne, James Garner, Tab Hunter, Joe DiMaggio, each in his own way appreciating Nikki Gentry in a bathing suit or an evening gown or tennis clothes, either holding a racquet or a golf club or a baseball bat, cutting a ribbon, popping a cork, thrilling to an Oscar, or just plain leaning in and being glamorous, one eye to the camera, the other pretty interested in the goings-on in each and every photo. And that was just the west wall.

She had invited me in just for a second and shown me to the softest, most enveloping leather sofa—dyed, I was sure. Leather hardly comes in lavender. She then handed me a portfolio of pictures and clippings that chronicled *The Nikki Gentry Story* from New York's Barbizon to Fountain and Sweetzer, and left me surrounded by a loving fan club while she pranced into another room and took forever to put away her panties.

I was home.

I decided to start a careful conversation.

"Do you know Joe DiMaggio?" Not quite tilting my head around the corner and into the hall.

"He's a baseball player. Would you like something? All I can offer you is tea or champagne."

"No, thanks."

"Chauch Hamilton sent a lovely bottle of Dom Perignon to my table at La Rue's."

"I'm fine."

"Do you know him?"

"Joe DiMaggio?"

"Chauch Hamilton."

"No."

"He's very sweet. Tea's almost ready," said Nikki, reappearing in the living room.

"Tell me, what part of England are you from?"

"*England?* Are you crazy?"

I'd frightened her again, and in her own home.

"No, no, I just thought . . ."

Again she whipped, and scampered into the apartment primeval.

"If I sound British to you, then you must be crazy," mused Nikki softly, matter-of-factly, from the safety of what I took to be the dark side of a bush, but was probably the kitchen. "I'm from Ne*brahs*ka."

Tea arrived.

"Do you like my eyes in *that* picture?" she inquired. Taming some, I thought, not eating out of my hand exactly, but slipping her heretofore aloof and sequestered parts if not next to me, certainly near me on the all-enveloping lavender leather sofa. She flopped a hoof. "Or better in *this* one."

I moved not one muscle—best plan in a strange forest—and made it my business to concentrate on the sixteen-by-twenty portfolio that defined Nikki Gentry and enveloped my lap. I focused on a blaze of hunger. . . .

No contest.

"I like your eyes in all of them," I admitted, and felt myself inch toward the Bogarter I was almost certain lay within.

"You're very sweet. Do you think you could drop me at the psychologist in Beverly Hills at three? And I have a few short errands after that. Or I could call a cab."

" I CAN'T fuckin' begieve it," said Rusty.

"You like?" I asked.

We stood on the sidewalk on Hayworth, a few car lengths from the entrance to the Clifford Apartments, and I was showing off.

"I'm hip! It looks brand-new, man!"

"I know. Under twenty bucks, too."

"No shit?"

"No shit. Earl Scheib, $19.95."

"And I love the color!"

"Forest-green. They overlapped a little on the chrome, but with a little lacquer thinner and a Q-tip . . ."

"It looks brand-new."

"It does."

"It looks brand fuckin' new, man. Too bad your clutch is made outta Cream of fuckin' Wheat, and when you come right down to it it's still the same piece 'a shit with a new paint job." The old tee-hee, and he fell all over himself, and I grabbed him around the neck and he pretended he was being choked.

CUT TO: Poolside, minutes later.

"Do you think?" I asked.

"Only when you stand directly under the sun, man, and there ain't a fuckin' thing on God's green earth you can do about it."

"Shit," I said.

"In six months you'll look like Fred MacMurray's father."

"Fuck you."

"Hey, man, I'll let you in on a little secret. Your old dad's checkin' out, too. See here?" Rusty carefully lifted the left side of his forelock, returned it to its rightful place, then lifted the right and returned same. "It's all in the hair comb."

"You think?"

"Most definitely! C'mere."

I scootched my chaise.

"Don't worry," he confided, burrowing. "Nobody's lookin'. I been wantin' to do this for a month." He began to nudge my hair forward. "Don't worry. I'm not gonna pull anything. You can't afford it."

"Very funny."

He moved my hair down and around in front. "I call it the bgow wave."

"The blow wave?"

"Exactly. You don't have to comb it. You just bgow it in pgace."

"Hysterical."

Rusty sat up.

I sat up.

Rusty looked at me. Awestruck.

I looked at Rusty. Naked.

Poolside was sparsely populated, for it was a weekday and the civilian population had gone to business, while those of us in The Business had gone to play as we lay in wait.

He straightened. *"Hey!"* said Rusty.

I moved not one muscle. "You're shouting."

"Man!" said Rusty.

"Shhhhhhh."

"I don't ask you to trust your old dad!" Whereupon he took me by the hand and led me upstairs into my apartment, through the living room, directly into the bathroom, and placed me in front of the mirror. He stood behind me, arms akimbo, and peered over my left shoulder.

"You think?" I asked.

"No, champ. I don't think. I *know.*"

"Yeah?"

"Very fuckin' Steve McQueen, man!"

LATER, I showered and shaved and shampooed and combed down and around, and called Nikki Gentry for the hell of it, and we made a quick trip from her apartment to Schwab's and back for eye shadow because it was early evening and she was pressed for time.

xviii
• • •

Sometimes I wonder if Stan knows who I am. If anybody knows who a person is, it should be a person's agent.

I'd gotten off work at eleven, punched out, and made it to the Raincheck, where, with the help of a little hand-eye coordination, Rusty and I took thirteen bucks off some new guy named Lawrence in liar's poker.

I pulled down my bed covers and checked with my answering service. Actor-Dial, which has a nice ring to it. I often joke around with the personnel.

"Call your agent, Johnny Bruno." It was Naomi. A genuine Lauren Bacall sound-alike.

"If it's nighttime it must be Naomi."

"Uh-huh."

"Hi, Naomi."

"Hi, Johnny Bruno," she said in a voice that most certainly came from under the covers.

"What time did that come in, light of my life?"

"That'll be the day. Sixish. Smells like an audition to me. Go get 'em, tiger. Nothing else for you. I'll keep 'em crossed."

I promised myself to run down to Actor-Dial on Sunset and Vine one of these lonely nights and take a look-see and maybe go for coffee.

I lit a cigarette and let it dangle.

It better be for the lead.

An effective way to get to sleep without screwing up one's daydreams is to snuggle under the covers and pretend one is dodging bullets.

STAN STRUGGLED with the word. "Pe-ri-phial, it says here. *Ramona?*"

"Peripheral?" I suggested, cradling the receiver between my neck and my shoulder, Day at a Glance opened to what promised to be a significant page of *The Johnny Bruno Story*. Pen at the ready.

"That's it. The two Lopez brothers, it says here, periphial slime."

"Slime?"

"Yeah."

". . . ."

"Right away you're gonna take it personal, am I right? Is that what I hear in *The Big Silence of 1962*, starring Johnny Bruno over the title—although I could swear I felt a sigh bustin' my chops over the ear waves. I need a sighing client like I need a dog act. It's a regular how-da-ya-call-it . . ."

"Heavy."

"Don't be a putz.* Get a pencil. Manny Lopez, thirtyish, slime, Paramount, twelve-twenty, Room twelve, Building B. You'll go, you'll do, you'll knock 'em on their asses and make a silk purse awreddy!"

S C H M U C K,+ I said to myself as I approached the Main Gate. The heart bell tinkles regardless.

Little children stumbled over one another inside my tummy as I clutched the script and moved softly down the hall from Room twelve, Building B, Paramount, Marathon off Melrose, where eight Johnny Bruno look-alikes appeared to be memorizing the carpet, and that was only the twelve-twenty group. The children and I went directly to the men's. It was vacant. I locked the door behind me. I shook out my wrists and flapped my arms and blubbered my lips and let my head hang down, then hang left and back and right and down again. Claire crossed my mind as I performed an excellent "Uuuhhhggg" into the mirror—which would have made Phoebe's night—in order to loosen up and tell the truth, till I resembled a terminal gorilla.

*Less than a schmuck
+More than a putz

I turned and leaned against the sink and thumbed the script back to front.

How much fun it would be, I thought to myself—easier, too, for some unknown reason—to say, as it says here in the tag on page sixty . . .

Farraday lifts his glass.

> FARRADAY
> I'm afraid this is good-bye.
> (reassuring)
> Time for you to patch things up with that big lug back in Wisconsin.
> (reflecting)
> A cop's life isn't what it's cracked up to be . . .
> (pausing)

Linda looks down, then out and away; eventually she meets Farraday's gaze.

> FARRADAY
> (continuing)
> We'll always have Aspen.

FADE OUT.

And I turned and said as much to the mirror.

And turned again and leaned against the sink and thumbed front to back.

What fun it would be, rather than . . .

Putting a gun to Linda's head.

                              MANNY
Shut up and drive.

... as it says here on page forty-eight.

SPECIAL AGENT CHIP FARRADAY, it says here on page one, thirtyish, determined, kicks the living shit out of what appears to be the less verbal of the slimy LOPEZ BROTHERS. In on forty-eight, out on forty-nine.

What the fuck's he doing in Aspen anyway if a cop's life isn't what it's ... ?

It occurred to me I was too relaxed.

They came for me.

And I blew it.

That's all.

I waltzed into the Inner Office and chatted up a snowstorm with what appeared to be the less verbal half of Mount Rushmore on the other side of the desk, and I blew it. I'm more than a putz, and I'll never work again.

WE DIDN'T even get to go to Aspen. We shot the "Snow Bank" episode of *Undercover, Undercover* on Stage 28.

Manny's talkative brother, Pedro Lopez, was a Greek named Paulie Majoris, who hailed from Pittsburgh and used to be a professional wrestler till he retired into acting, where he works all the time and does his own stunts. He taught me how to fall on concrete without giving myself a face-lift. He'd heard of Nikki Gentry, but he'd never met her. You learn a lot about someone when you spend ten hours in the backseat of an inconspicuous sedan. I'm exaggerating. The director's name was Abner.

Rʀʀɪɪɪɴɴɴɢ...

I'd just gotten under the covers and was so tired I barely knew myself. Rusty always says that. "Man, I'm so tired of this fuckin' town I don't even know myself."

Rrriiinnng ...

Earlier in the evening he'd hung a sign on my back that I carried to and fro between keypunch and locater file for an hour—ɪ'ᴍ ɢᴏɪɴɢ ʙᴀʟᴅ—and I'd still have it on if Bobbi Jean hadn't damn near pulled a hip joint laughing and pointing and whippling. Then I hid Rusty's lunch in the crapper, third stall, and we laughed so hard we didn't know ourselves.

Rrriiinnng ...

"Mmmmm."

"Johnny?"

"Mmmmm."

"Nikki."

"Mmmmm! Hi!"

"Is this Johnny Bruno?"

"Absolutely."

"It's Nikki. Do you know anything about heaters?"

"Heaters?"

"Heaters and pilot lights and that sort of thing. This house is freezing and your line's been busy."

"I was checking with my service."

"I just arrived home from a rather nice party, actually—at Bob Evans's house—and my heater won't turn on and this house is freezing. I'm very susceptible to colds. I don't know if I told you that."

So we went for coffee.

Nikki and I.

I lit her light, she threw on a mink, and while the museum was heating up, we went for coffee at one-thirty A.M.

Nikki and Johnny.

The Chez Paulette coffeehouse on Sunset just west of La Cienega sits in an arcade, and one can sit either inside or outside. We sat inside. Brrrr. The place is run by Max, who looks and talks like Napoleon. His mother makes the pastries. Coffee is twenty-five cents and worth it. My favorite of all the posters on the wall is a huge one of Delores del Rio (*Maria Candelaria*), looking down on what appears to be an ice cream cone but is meant to be a flower. They have a waitress named Sally Kellerman who's very abrupt and will never make it in the restaurant business, but, oh, those soft guitars.

Nikki toyed with her cinnamon stick and sparkled all over the place.

I cooled it, and talked beginnings. I skimmed the high points of my gig on *Hotline: Hawaii.*

"Oh?" said Nikki, now rapidly stirring her hot cider.

"You had a nice time with Jock Jason? I had a dreadful time with Jock Jason."

"Oh?" I asked, cooling it.

"Oh, yes, I know Jock Jason very well. He's not a nice man."

"Really?" Really cooling it.

"Well, my dear, he grabbed me like *this* . . ."

I switched my cup.

". . . at a wonderful party at Jayne Mansfield's house. My back was turned to him and he grabbed me and jerked me around . . ."

I wanted her on the spot.

". . . that's very hostile. I think he's queer. See this mark on my arm . . ."

Extraordinary arm.

". . . that's your friend, Jock Jason. Mind you, this was two weeks ago, and that mark should be gone by now. I had lunch with my attorney today. Lloyd Gerber. Do you know Lloyd? He's a very important attorney . . ."

Although I was a little tired.

". . . Lloyd said if I was still having trouble sleeping by the end of the week, we should do something about it."

Not that tired, really.

"I'm exhausted," she added.

"I'm *exhausted!*" shivered Nikki as she bundled her mink around her shoulders and trotted just a little ahead of me in tall heels over cobblestones from the car through the courtyard, three steps up to her front door.

Around her pink naked shoulders is the phrase that came

to mind as I strode behind her. *And I'll never be cold no more*, I mused. *The Rainmaker.* Hepburn and Lancaster.

She fumbled through her purse, found her key, inserted it in the proper hole, and opened a crack. "You were very sweet to warm up my apartment." She flickered in the half light. "Night." And disappeared into the woods.

"Night."

I took a drive.

Lo and behold, DuPar's, Farmers Market, Third and Fairfax, is an all-nighter.

I'D NEVER seen the inside of Elizabeth Arden's on Rodeo between Dayton and Brighton before, but I'd always been curious because my understanding is that it's for women only. So I took a peek. Turns out, a facial is a facial, a manicure is a manicure, and a pedicure is what Fiarenza does to your toes to make your feet attractive. Nikki was fairly bowled over when I mentioned I'd never heard of one. "You cahn't be serious." Besides, everything happens upstairs. So I walked over to Cañon Drive and shot the breeze with Walt for a couple of hours till they finished her up, and talked him out of a double-dip lime ice. Naturally, he'd never met her, but he'd seen her *pitcher*.

xix
• • •

The situation was unacceptable, I thought, as I drove around and around and around the block, keeping one eye peeled on the entrance to the Bernie Safire Hair Salon each time it peeked back at me from the corner of Rodeo Drive and Brighton Way. Left on Rodeo, left on Brighton, left on Beverly . . . so when she pokes her new head out the door she won't be forced to scurry willy-nilly across the street into oncoming traffic, rather heavy in Beverly Hills this time of day . . . left on Santa Monica . . . Unacceptable is hardly the word for it. One audition in four months is outrageous. Stan will be sorry.

" I JUST DON'T think he knows who I am," I confided to Hal Shiffman, head of the considerably well-known Shiffman Agency. Shifty himself in the flesh.

He was a portly man. And short, judging from where

the lip of his desk met him just below the nipples. If one is aware, one thinks of Porky Pig. If one is stupid, one dwells on it.

"Who took these pictures?" he asked.

A stout man. And young.

"They're old."

Younger than I.

"You need new pictures."

And very businesslike. He plopped them.

"That's easy," I said, showing confidence because that's what they look for.

He leaned way back in his thick leather chair, with his arms up and his baby fingers entwined at the back of his head. Stan scrunches. And he took from his mouth what appeared to be a pretty expensive cigar. You don't see that many pinkie rings. "Too bad you weren't around last week."

"Now why is that?" As in pray tell. A little cockiness never hurt Aunt Rose.

"Too late. Cast already. A thing at MGM."

"*See?*" I pleaded in a forgotten octave, leaning my blow wave over his desk as far as possible without falling off my chair or eating the blotter. Hardly Monty Clift, I thought, as I felt myself tumble, from warrior, lover, magician, and king, into the kicking booties of a Baby Sandy. "That's what I *mean!*" I gushed.

The Shiffman Agency regarded me.

And I recovered like a champ.

In quick time I leaned back, calculated the height of

my chair back, threw an arm over it. I studied the potted plant in order to gather myselves, then eased my gaze upward, enjoying *Brief Encounter* with secretary separated by glass. Her nameplate read Ciel, which I took to mean hot for Cecelia. Thought better of putting my foot on the big little man's desk. Instead grinned at the many recognizable hopeful faces on the wall, including former Vice President Richard M. Nixon—who I was prepared to like—autographed.

"You got a quality. No question about it," he said, sucking his cigar. "Honey, find my lighter! Trouble is, I already got three of you."

"*Am I intruding?*"

I was on my back in my bed contemplating The Undoing of Nikki G.

Elmer Gantry is indelicate.

"*If I'm intruding I trust you'll tell me so's I don't make a fool of myself. Am I right, kid?*"

"*Right Burt. You're not intruding.*"

"*Because if I am . . .*"

How many times do I have to say it? "*I have a minute.*"

"*Then take your hands out from under the covers and lay them down at your sides. That's it. Nice as you please. See, unlike you, kid, I can't do seventeen things at once, much less two.*" Understanding smile.

"*What's that supposed to mean?*"

"*Kid, I see it in the stars!*" He waved his arms and

waltzed around the room, stopping short of the mirror over the chest of drawers, into which he stared. *"Armageddon!"* He's so dramatic. *"As sure as God created the heavens above!"* Eyes up. *"The earth right here!"* He gathered his fists into my bedroom, then flattened his palms, glared at the shag carpet, and let them drop. *"And hellfire below!"* Simple, simple, says Phoebe. *"The point is, kid . . . I got a problem."* He's a master of the quick recovery. I'll give him that.

"You?"

"Yeah."

"You *got a problem?"*

"For a change."

"That's a switch."

"Got a minute?"

"Shoot."

"See, I feel like I'm workin' overtime, and at the same time you're hard to reach these days." Beat-pause. *"By the look on your face, kid, you recognize that as a contradiction."*

I was not in the mood for thinking. *"Sort of."*

He cocked a little and pointed an index finger—for a minute I thought he was going to tap his head like Stan. *"A step in the right direction, kid."*

"You haven't exactly pushed the issue," I stated, which was the truth.

"Who's on first?"

"I don't know."

"He's on third. Be that as it may . . . I got a problem."

Jesus, it was getting late. *"Being?"*

"You got me seein' out of other people's eyes and hearin' out of other people's ears, and it's gettin' so . . . "

"Go on."

"It's gettin' so I hardly recognize myself."

I thought about that one for a minute. *"Where do we go from here?"*

He grew dim and faint, and I strained to see and hear as he strode into the mirror of my mind, and I recognized a line J. J. Hunsecker once said to a confused Tony Curtis in *Sweet Smell of Success:*

"I'm a schoolboy. Teach me. Teach me . . . "

XX

• • •

Phoebe tells the class that it's incumbent upon us to bring to the surface and deal with the seven-eighths of the iceberg that usually remains submerged. I'm so glad I'm in the advanced class. She also says that in order to create true drama, there must be something at stake.

Claire hasn't changed a bit. She'd crept into The Little Theatre Off Melrose while class was in progress, which sets Phoebe's hair on end even more than usual. There's supposed to be a rule. We all abide by it unless one of us is stricken with acute pellagra. She's been gone for a hundred and fifty years and still can't abide by the goddamn rules.

She wore a maxiskirt, gray with slits that swished, and dark suede flat-heeled boots that bunched, and a mighty maroon sweater with a cowl neck, and oversized glasses that made perfect sense.

I'm convinced that if the late Mrs. Van Horn hadn't

given me a little wave as she edged along the far wall, and I hadn't given her a big one back and screeched my folding chair and mouthed how sorry I was to hear about the death of Eleanor Roosevelt, and given the teacher the back of my head during her critique on *Sweet Bird of Youth*, it would never have been my turn in the barrel.

She put me up there with Judy.

Las Vegas Judy doesn't even know how to say hello. I say hi to her now and then just to watch her wink an eye and snap her fingers and stare at my forehead. And now I'm stuck with her for sensory awareness in front of Claire and everybody. I wonder if she's a real redhead.

"*Explooore* each other's hands . . ." Phoebe moaned on. "Sense of touch . . . awareness of textures . . ."

Judy prodded.

"*Mooove* to the forearms and the shoulders . . . sense of smell . . . awareness of aromas . . ."

And sniffed at me like a tall puppy.

"*Eeease* to necks and hair and faces . . . sense of taste . . ."

And nibbled at my cheek for the better part of fifteen minutes, as if I needed a wake-up call.

Phoebe concluded Judy was a walking rim shot, which got a big yuk, and that I'd rather go down on a woman than fuck her, which flummoxed me in front of the entire class—who nodded sagely. I'd never thought about it in those terms. I didn't know whether to kiss Phoebe or kill myself or kill Phoebe and kiss myself.

"You haven't changed a bit, Johnny B.," Claire said as we came together in the lobby.

"You, too."

"Bullshit, but don't stop."

"Lemon meringue, am I right?"

"And French apple."

"You remembered."

"You, too."

"So . . . ?"

"Yeah . . . !"

Coffee arrived.

We ordered pie.

"I was sure sorry to hear about Eleanor Roosevelt," I began, in case she hadn't seen and heard it the first time.

"Some people should be allowed to live forever."

"Who said that?" I became aware I tend to hunch when I'm with Claire.

"I did."

"You mean just *now?*"

"Yeah." And she tends to sit back.

"Wow. So. Are you guys here for a while?"

"We better be, we just bought the most expensive house in Malibu."

"Really?" Location, I thought.

"Seems like it."

"Wow."

"If you're going to say wow all night, I'm having my pie to go."

"What does old Lucky do exactly?"

"He's at UCLA."

"A teacher?"

"A doctor."

"A doctor?"

"A surgeon."

Ben Casey, I thought.

"Recently from Columbia Presbyterian, currently ensconced in heart research for the masses at his alma mater, where he was an all-sports hero a hundred years ago. Principally transplants on dogs. Is this an interview?"

I liked the way she said that. Is this an interview? And then she smiled.

Pie arrived.

I noticed once again as she lifted a fork full of fluffy stuff the barely noticeable smattering of the lightest of light bronze fuzz between Claire's knuckles and the natural bent of her fingers, and decided to drop my keys on the floor.

"Ooops."

I retrieved them.

She smiled.

I smiled.

"You're a naughty boy, Johnny B."

"Who? Me?"

"Eat your pie. Who are you dating these days?"

"Who am I dating?"

"Uh-huh."

"Nikki Gentry."

"Nikki Gentry?"

"Nikki Gentry. Is this an interview?"

Claire poised her fork in outer space and snapped into a somewhat vicious and certainly overblown imitation, elongating her already long neck, cocking her head, flashing her teeth, opening wide and looking at nothing.

"Did you ever get your eyes examined?" she asked, digging into her crust.

"Me?"

"Remember? We talked about it."

I ALLOWED as how I had never seen a Facel Vega up close before, and Claire allowed as how she had never laid eyes on a forest-green '51 Chevy but she wouldn't let it stand in our way. "We'll do it again one day anyway," she said in the parking lot, and gave me a kiss on the cheek in the middle of my handshake, so I gave her one also. She'd pretty much decided that she was going to attend class on a visit-only basis, if Phoebe would stand still for such an arrangement, and then only once in a while because of the distance.

DR. BEN CASEY slouched in my brain, yet my heart beat wildly, for there was always the risk that Nikki Gentry would whirl.

"Let's have a look at that bruise," I said.

To my great pleasure, she merely turned. "The one that refuses to go away?"

"That one."

"The one I sustained when your friend, Jocko Jason, practically pummeled me at that party at—"

"Yeah, that one."

She had just arrived home from a screening and reception at the Directors Guild of America for a movie she was perfect for and should have been in.

I had arrived moments later, and as luck would have it, bent the right thing and the toilet stopped running.

We were on the couch.

For the duration.

Volume III of *Nikki G.* lapped us.

"Don't you think acting is a rather strange profession for a man?" she inquired of the air. "It seems so . . . I don't know . . . feminine . . ."

She was in a trailing mood.

"Feminine?"

"That's what Sy thinks . . ."

"Sy?"

"Dr. Simon Taubman. You remember, you dropped me off . . . he's very wise . . ."

"Let's have a look at that bruise."

"Okay."

Gingerly, she lifted the half sleeve of an elegant slip of a something.

"I'm merely going to squiggle my fingertips very gently

around the affected area without coming in contact with the actual wound," I stated reassuringly, straining my eyes for signs of violence—also finding myself in a trailing mood . . . aware of textures . . . yet fearful of frightening the patient. "Do you understand?"

She looked away. "I think so . . ."

"Good."

Painstakingly, our hero—his body rigid with care—performed in this manner for many minutes, and managed with professional aplomb to ignore the kink in his lower back and with surgical precision to avoid dumping Volume III through the considerable spread of his legs.

"I may ask you to stroke my shoulder . . . you know . . . above my bruise . . . before I go sleepy-bye . . ."

She neither spun nor whipped. As if through molasses, Nikki's heart-shaped face descended toward both our laps, and her soft head hung for a moment as if in the midst of decision.

"Do you like my hair this length, or that?" she asked her portfolio before admitting to being rather tired now.

FADE IN:

THE FOREST.

SHE
(innocently)
Why are you removing my dress?

                    HE
                (absently)
To stroke your shoulder.
                    SHE
                (fearfully)
Is that necessary, Doctor?
                    HE
                (flatly)
I'm afraid so.
                    SHE
                (resignedly)
I see.

                    HE
Bend your elbow.
                    SHE
I cahn't.
                    HE
Try.
                    SHE
Ow.
                    HE
                (reassuringly)
That wasn't so bad now, was it?
                    SHE
You're removing my bra.
                    HE
Exactly.
                    SHE
It's in the back.
                    HE
Thank you.

We HEAR murmurings not uncommon to woodsy areas.

                              SHE

Mmmm . . .

                              HE

Lift this foot.

                              SHE
                      (not without concern)
Careful . . . my dress . . . it was a gift from . . .

                              HE

Shhhhh.

                              SHE

Oleg Cassini.

                              HE

Now this one.

                              SHE

Mmmmm . . .

CAMERA PANS up, down, and all over the place TO
REVEAL shades of lushness and good fortune and comes
finally to rest on what we dimly perceive to be a lavender
clearing in the remotest nook, as we . . .

CUT TO:

A bed of many leaves.

                              SHE
                           (airily)
Where in the world are you going . . . ?

                              HE
                         (hypnotically)
I'm going to tilt this leg now.

He does so.

                        HE
                   (continuing)
          Like so. And this one . . .

He does so.

                        HE
                   (continuing)
          Like so.
                        SHE
                   (to the sky)
          You're terribly thorough, Doctor.
                        HE
                   (to the stars)
          Don't move.

DISSOLVE TO:

xxi
• • •

PORTS.

CAMERA FINDS A BLACK DOT on the horizon. It appears to be moving toward our lens, growing ever larger, much in the manner of Omar Sharif ambling stoically through the shimmer toward a dilemma-ridden Lawrence of Arabia, and though hardly astride a one-humped camel, MARGIE COSGROVE looms enormous.

"Hi," she said.

"Hellew," said the other.

"Hey!" said I as the three of us stood there like bold numbers on an old calendar in somebody's basement. "Margie, say hello to Nikki. Nikki, say hello to Margie."

"Hi," she repeated.

"Hellew," repeated the other, extending herself through mink. "I'm Nikki *Gentry*." Preferring the more complete introduction. "A friend from yesteryear . . ." she trailed.

"Hah," began Margie.

"Hey!" said I.

"I'm Marie *Cosgrove*," she concluded.

"Join us, won't you?" is the phrase that fell out of my mouth and dribbled down my chin, for I was dull-witted and weary of improvisation, and I wasn't sure to whom I was directing the question.

Or what I wanted.

Phoebe used to growl, "What does the character *want* in the scene? What is your *action*?" Urgent that one play a strong action, translated into civilian: what do I want to do *to* her or *for* her. I can just hear Phoebe: "*Which* her is *your* problem?" Also: "One must not, *cannot* play self-pity." Highly unattractive and "Who gives a shit?" she'd add.

I chose to take the helm.

"Please," said Nikki. "Do sit down." So we did. "Perhaps I shall join you for a short while . . ." she mused as she slipped into the booth and pressed the entirety of her next to my thigh and into the sofa of my mind. "I'm with this dreadful little man—no, don't look—who *says* he's a producer . . . he keeps talking about some jungle movie in the Philippines . . . but I have my doubts . . . He actually grabbed me by the wrist . . . He wants me to be empress of the jungle or something . . ."

Margie looked on from twenty thousand feet across the table.

"Listen . . . let me give you my number . . . in Beverly Hills . . ."

I felt awash in old habits as I anticipated the helpless-

ness of the species . . . Yet . . . I chose to modulate my behavior, not to leap into my purse.

". . . I don't have a single thing to write on . . ."

Rather to unzip it slowly, rummage casually.

". . . Perhaps we can get together . . ."

"Coffee would be fun," I modulated.

My fingers came in contact with the list of Margie's kin
and the stuff of Claire, and I took some time. Never ne-
glect one's immediate atmosphere, right, Phoebe? For a
simple texture may hold the key to the scene. Eventually
I removed pen and checkbook, and backslid as I yanked
a deposit slip and shoved it in her direction, successfully
forsaking the soggy cocktail napkin which tends to blur.

". . . Although as a rule I seldom drink coffee, I don't
know if you remember . . ."

"I remember."

She wrote in a scamper, served it up with fingers aghast.

"That sure is one helluva coat," announced Margie,
closing the distance.

"Oh, this . . . thank you . . . yes . . . I've had this for
centuries . . . you remember, Johnny . . ."

"I remember."

Nikki flickered. "I wonder if you might run me home.
I think this guy's a creep. If your friend could wait or
something—I don't drive, you know—I won't keep him
long . . . or maybe your friend could drive me . . ."

I smiled at my friend.

"Hell, my car's in Fresno."

"Not tonight," I said, and wondered if awareness of aroma and taste remains constant over time.

"Of course not," said Nikki. "Well, I guess I'll just have to fend for myself," she added with a lilt.

The fawn slipped out of the booth as if she had been photographed slipping into the booth and the film had been reversed, for slipping in is a more fluid motion than slipping out.

All those still in awe, stand up and be counted, I said to myself.

We clasped.

"Nikki Gentry," I stated.

"Mmmmm...?" she asked, not unhappy with the ring of it.

"I crown thee *Empress of the Jungle.*"

One can imagine the exit.

Miss Daisy Mae of 1953 swizzled her ice.

"You got a stiff neck?"

"Who? Me? Just a little kink."

"You're gettin' up there, kid, like me. I give great massages. For two cents I'd come over there—"

"No, no, it's . . . I'm fine."

"I think that's what Harley likes best about me, at least that's what he says."

"Your son," I guessed, halfway back.

"My current. You're thinkin' of Harvey."

"Your third. Husband, I mean."

"Fourth, and I'm about ready to tell him to stick it where the sun don't shine. I bet that mink coat set somebody back a few massages. Where the hell's she from, anyway?"

"London."

"I figured."

"It's a gift."

"The coat?"

"The art of massage."

"Hey . . ."

"What?"

"You gave me my first orchid. 'Member?"

"I do," I said. And did. And thought to myself: *what an excellent time for a segue, no matter how clumsy.* "You'll get a kick out of this." I chuckled. "These two actors are walking down Sunset Boulevard, see, and all of a sudden they see this other guy topple from the top of a twenty-story building. Topple, topple, topple, fightin' all the way. And sittin' there at a red light is this truck with twelve mattresses stacked up on the back, and lo and behold, the guy lands directly in the middle of the goddamn mattresses, bounces off, lands on his feet on the sidewalk, brushes himself off, and walks away nice as you please. One actor turns to the other actor and says, 'Man, that's what I call luck!' And the other actor says, 'No, man. Charlton Heston, *that's* luck!'"

"Turns to which guy?"

"The actor."

"Turns to . . ."

"The other actor."

"Wait a minute . . ."

"Turns to the other actor and *says*—"

"How come Charlton Heston?"

"Whither goest thou?"

Quo Vadis
MGM, 1951

"Let it be wonderful or let it be awful so long as
it is uncommon!"

Quo Vadis
MGM, 1951

xxii

• • •

I predict color TV will revolutionize the industry, that Mickey Mantle will hit his five hundredth career home run next season, and that Chris George will be the leading rat in *The Rat Patrol* because I got sweaty on the audition.

However, I'm thrilled, and indebted to National Foods, and a little scared.

"You'll go, you'll do, you'll be a real-person for a change," which was the dress category for the audition, as opposed to casual, upscale-casual, upscale, or upscale-upscale. Fortunately for me since my budget doesn't allow for a whole lot of scales.

Crispy-Toasties is a giant account, and Madison Avenue only knows how many real-persons they saw. Thirty, maybe forty. "Left profile please. Right profile please. Straight on and say hi! to everybody."

"Hi!" To everybody.

It's the height that scares me some.

One eventually gets used to rubber pellets, Midge assured me as I sat in the makeup chair and she stuffed them up my nose, and I'm sure it's true. They're only the size of a pea, for crying out loud, that one might purchase in a pod at the Arrow Market. In fact, you could probably use peas if you ran out of pellets. And one can relax because they don't suck up far enough to choke a person to death, and don't let anybody tell you differently, Midge emphatically stated, shaking her long blond hair out of her big brown eyes. Large peas, thankfully. XLs. See how they widen the nostrils, I said silently to the mirror. One must remember to breathe through the mouth, so one doesn't pop one in the middle of an otherwise good take. Obviously I'm aware of that. Midge hardly needed to remind me. She wore no bra under something thin and stylish as she took away my coffee cup and handed me a slab of sponge rubber to wedge between my gum and upper lip. That really alters the situation, I would have told her if I could. I watched us through the mirror as she glued hair onto my back and fitted me with what we in The Business refer to as a fright wig.

I had never seen Arizona before.

Much less embraced it border to border in one gulp.

"I love you," I said.

"I love you, too," said Jesus, as I dangled fifty feet or so above the desert floor and overlooked the magnificence of all that cactus from a cute basket that came not quite to my waist.

"Do you recognize me?"

"Sort of."

My action, I thought to myself, is much like the chicken crossing the road. To swing from one mesa to another via a tiny pulley from an invisible wire dressed like a vine.

"I apologize for wanting the makeup lady."

With nothing to break my fall but eighteen ounces of Crispy Toasties, label to the lens, in one paw and a prize in the other. That's what shrinks my scrotum. Any fool can growl and wave at America and hope to Christ the country will bend a little and buy the concept of an Easter Monkey.

Dear Mom,

Shooting the big one in Yuma. Wish you were here.

I LIKE very much the manner in which Henri ate her hand.

He plucked it, as if from thin air, proclaimed the banns to the chandelier—a hosanna of fuis and puis and cghughs and Mon Dieus. He held a small engagement party, then eloped with and subsequently ravaged the hand and the wrist and tickly underbelly of the forearm, which by now were involved in a trip to St.-Tropez and only remotely connected to the new lady, buckling in the foyer at Cyrano's on The Strip.

We were escorted with fervor and alacrity to a table by the fire. Henri's look to her, as he assisted, was one of secret sorrow and passion remembered, before he nipped off to the bar.

And it's cheap, too.

"Happy birthday, Ev."

"Well, sweetie, I'm thrilled to be in Hollywood. Charles wishes he could be here, too." She shook her head up and down, earrings all over the place as I attempted to light her cigarette. "Yes, I *am!*"

"How about an old-fashioned with Early Times, heavy on the sugar?" I asked.

It's in the round, is Cyrano's, and nice-noisy as opposed to noisy-noisy or nice-nice, and by some acoustical quirk that no one in The Business should even question, let alone try to comprehend—we have no physicists here—sound is fickle. Conversations that are barely discernible across the table skitter around the inner circumference of the room in ever ascending circles, down the fireplace, and up through one's butter plate across a crowded room. Don't ask me.

"I'll have a Tanqueray on the rocks," answered Claire quietly from some forty-odd feet away.

I chose to stretch.

Minimally, casually.

To take in for a split second my immediate surroundings.

Alcove bar over my left shoulder, busy-nice.

Kitchen busy-busy to my right, and came semicircularly to appreciate the atmosphere as a whole, thereby to discover specifically:

Dr. Lucky Van Horn was surgically handsome.

Erect as a bullet.

With the slitty eyes of an aging linebacker.

"I'd love one!" enthused Ev.

The Mrs. wore a loose-fitting light gray sheath with a V-neck and no glasses, and seemed arched in his direction across the table, much in the manner of I with her.

"Me, too, Ev."

"Honey, you don't drink old-fashioneds."

"Darling, have the London broil," suggested Claire.

"The London broil is the best thing on the menu," I reiterated to Ev.

"And the Cyrano salad, and save room for a mocha frost," tinkled Claire from my small fork.

"It *comes* with the Cyrano salad," I asserted.

"You really *do* have to raise your voice in here, don't you, sweetie!"

She lightly touched his hand, which refused to give, and the length of her rose and made its way toward the powder room in the foyer.

"Let's see if I can't rustle up a waiter," said I, rising to the occasion.

Through the use of a sophisticated listening device—stoppage of breath—the crafty saboteur listened for and heard a flush through walls, detected a faucet connected to a faucet, a towel dispenser to its sister. He surmised: she has long legs, I have long legs . . . one, two, three . . .

We exited rest rooms in unison.

She touched my arm.

She stirs confusion.

"Of course!" She stood opposite me now, naked-eyed-blue and widely smiling, eminent in heels and makeup. "I caught your act when you came in. Is that your mom? What fun! We'll come say happy birthday."

Her shoes were red, I noticed as she moved away, and her ankles were of the etched variety, which speaks a lingo of its own.

"Dr. Quisenberry says, 'Evelyn, as long as you keep those ears good and washed out every month without fail, why, you won't have any trouble at *all* with your hearing in your advanced years!' It's a wax buildup. According to Dr. Quisenberry. Bruno has the same thing. A wax buildup." She nodded three times in the affirmative. "Since he was a little boy!"

"Is that your real name? Bruno?" asked Claire as they stood over us.

"It's the acoustics, Mom."

"Bruno *what?*" She gave the world her little *interested* smile.

"Bruno *Sangenito,*" sang Ev.

"Very musical. Why on earth did you change it?"

"We have some friends in Florence," added the iron man. "Sorrento, I think their name is."

Ev giggled into her mocha frost.

"What?" I asked over mine.

It's infectious and I was insane.

"What?" I giggled. "What now?"

"That man . . ."

"Which?"

"Who just left. Your friend."

"Dr. Zorba?"

"Well, I've been staring at him all through supper, and until they sent Henry over with that Galliano, I could have sworn he was Burt Lancaster."

IN PER MO.	OUT PER MO.
Cafe Nunzio:	Food—0
Salary—$100.00	Clothes—0
Tips—$5.00	Apt.—$62.50
Unemployment Ins.—$160.00	Alfa-Romeo—$75.00
Diff. in rent betw.	Gas—$25.00
then and now—$12.50	Repairs—$75.00
	Class—$12.50
	Ent.—maybe $50.00
TOTAL:	TOTAL:
$277.50	$299.50

Thanks to shit-job number three, life doesn't add up.

Nobody sober lays a tip on the putz-martinet in the shiny blue gabardine with the minestrone shoes at his post behind the cash register under which he hoards continuous cups of undocumented soup for five hours. Nor does one normally collect hazard pay for escorting unsteady ladies and their drunken boyfriends out to the parking lot of a late evening, although it has had its compensations, and I don't miss the pool all that much.

You know who's lucky?

Sean Connery.

I should be working every day.

Everybody says so.

Phil at the Raincheck says I'm positively ripe for a series. Rusty says so, too. So does Jay. Las Vegas Judy says I'm a cross between Louis Prima and Sammy Davis, Jr. Don't ask. One can only imagine the drumroll as Little Red and I whipped back to the Bide-Awhile in a frenzied look-see for a mislaid G-string so she could segue home intact.

Naomi. Take Naomi, the mystery voice who turned out to be not exactly what the doctor ordered but is a very special person indeed, as is her friend, Ruby. Both say I'm a cross between David Janssen and Skippy Homeier, who *I* barely remember, and not to forget them when I'm famous. Fat chance.

David Janssen works all the time.

Ciel says I resemble Lee Marvin in the mouth, and Nikki needs her kitchen painted.

If only James Bond were American for a change.

I like Mr. Nunzio very much. And he likes me, speaking of luck. He almost broke my collarbone telling me what a valuable employee I was because I don't steal. "I luv dis kid, I luv dis kid." For my birthday he had the chef grill me a New York steak medium-rare, mixed me a Caesar salad with his bare hands, and gave me Exotica for the night.

Who I'd really like to be is Lenny Bruce.

MY CURRENT APARTMENT is a studio affair within step-counting distance of the Cafe Nunzio. I took Exotica's hand in mine on the way, but I could tell she wasn't bowled over by the idea, so I let go. What does one say to a foregone conclusion?

She unwrapped down to her panties and bra—black, lacy—before I could get my tie off, and sat quietly on my chenille bedspread. Long black hair and no smile. It occurred to me to laugh her into the sack.

Everybody who's hip digs Lenny Bruce. Lenny, as we call him.

"You'll get a kick out of this," I said, and went on to explain his relevance to society as a whole.

" 'What's shakin', baby?' he says to the goddamn *pope*! I've got every single one of his albums. 'Ya-da-ya-da-ya-da!' he yells up to the warden from the prison yard, who's really Hume Cronyn. 'Ya-da-ya-da-ya-da, Warden!' Then Hume Cronyn yells down, '*Never* mind those Louis Armstrong impressions, you're a *rotten* vicious criminal!' Can't you hear him? Then Father Flotsky says, just like Barry Fitzgerald, 'You're not a *bad* boy, Dutch . . .'

". . . anyway . . .

"... I don't do him that great, but he's a trip ..."

"No. It's good," she said.

" 'Son ... killing six children doesn't make anybody *bad*!' Can't you just hear him?"

" ... "

" 'Ya-da-ya-da, Fadda Flotsky ...' "

"Ready for another hit?"

"Sure. What's your real name?"

"Carolyn. What's yours?"

"Sangenito."

"Let's make love."

PHOEBE SAYS this town is loaded with talent, but what it's not loaded with is people who know how to put one foot in front of the other in terms of building a career. I was sure she was talking to me.

It's not that his office is located in the spacious new Buckeye Building on upper Sunset, and it has nothing to do with the celeb photos on the wall or the fuzzlet secretaries who apparently rotate. It's that Benny Bessmacher is young and trim—we've even dated some of the same women—and built his reputation on aggressive behavior. He smiles constantly, and is aware of me in a sense. He likes what he sees and agrees that pinstripe Stan Feinberg is on his last kishkas and for years I've been misrepresented.

I complimented Benny on his upscale glass desk and

the life-size oil portrait of himself directly in back of it which made him look like twins, and hit him with the facts *re* my current representation.

"Hey, it happens," he shrugged, and we came to a complete understanding.

It is customary to sign on the dotted line with the new bunch before one drops the old bunch, so one stands no chance of missing the Big One during the gap—true Hollywood legend.

We chatted for a while, mostly about broads.

Benny handed me an eleven-by-fourteen photo on quality paper.

"Check this out."

I checked it out.

"Gorgeous," I admitted.

"Is she not dynamite?"

We agreed.

"Dynamite. Is she yours?"

He got a little wistful. "A client."

"No shit?"

"Uh-huh."

"What's her name?"

"Bellybutton."

Cute, I thought. "What category?" I asked, and we shared a laugh.

"Pure Labrador retriever," he said, riveted to the photo. And he launched into the friendliest, most hyster-ical conversation about this very clever pooch who could actually fetch a bone from a three-meter diving board at the deep end of the pool. A potential gold mine.

We laughed and laughed.

Stan will be devastated.

I ENTERED the building on lower Hollywood Boulevard and stepped into the rickety elevator, hoping a cable would snap before we got to the third floor, for all my rehearsal time in the car on the way down had yielded bupkus.

It was nine and a half steps from the elevator door to the Feinberg Agency, which I'd never realized before.

"You don't wear a sweater in this weather?" Ramona asked, looking up from her little brown desk in the alcove. "He doesn't own a sweater," she explained to God.

"Wear a sweater!" yelled Stan from inside his small office, where he'd recognized my voice.

I moseyed in and stood opposite his scratchy brown desk and rested my fingertips there.

"You're leaving," he said.

"Huh?"

"Boychikal. Do I look by you like a Rip Van Winkler, I been asleep for fifty years? I don't recanize da look on a client's demeanor when I see sayonara?" He tapped his head three times, looked up at me and smiled. "So?"

"Yeah ... well ... I thought ..."

He sat back in his chair, still smiling, and made a steeple out of his hands. "So who ya goin' wit?"

"Uh . . . I thought . . . maybe . . . bennysmrrr . . ."

"*Who* da fuck?"

"Benny Bessmacher?"

"Mazel tov.* *Ramona!* Ya want coffee?"

"Uh . . . no . . . thanks. I mean thanks. Thanks for everything . . ."

Come to think of it, I thought, Stan smiles all the time, too.

"Hey," he said. "It happens."

*Good luck

xxiii

• • •

I could make my own movie.

If I knew how . . .

SERIES OF SHOTS (let's say):

A) The clock strikes noon.

B) Our hero stays in bed and thinks about how he could make a movie.

Screw it.

C) He enters the bathroom

D) His crossover faces yell from the mirror in the prison yard.

E) He punches his worthless shower head and decides to call Nikki to pop over and fix it.

It could be a comedy.

F) He is getting low on hair spray.

Or a tragedy.

G) For the life of him, he can't think of a series of shots for the rest of the day.

Or a slice of life.

H) Naomi says, "Nothing for you, cutie." Ruby says, "Hi, stranger," in the background.

Montages are a trip.

MONTAGE—NIGHT SEQUENCE:

Sherry from the Pancake Palace. I can barely read her number. And Heather from the agency. And—no, forget her. And Mary K., it looks like here. Or is it Merry? And what's-her-name from the bar at the Villa Frascati. And Jan, daytime *only* . . .

DISSOLVE TO:

A flurry of many empty calendar pages flicking off into space, signifying passage of time.

NEW SHOT.

"Br-o-o-o-no Sangenito! What da hell kind of a name is that? Don't tell me—Chinese. I knew you awreddy when you was Tarzan'a da Monkeys."

"You lost weight, I'll make coffee."

I WAS JAZZED!

"But I *don't!*" I yelled into Stan's ear. I could almost hear him jerk the receiver and stare at the mouthpiece.

"You'll *loin!*" He was jazzed, too. "I tol' 'em you was an expoit."

"An expert?"

"An expoit."

"I'll learn. You bet I'll learn. I want to learn. I've always wanted to learn to ride."

"Like the wind, I tol' 'em."

I just never had the time, is all.

"Ya got two weeks. A half-assed actor can learn to fly by his own hands in two weeks."

Not since Ev and I did once around the pony trail.

One enjoys hearing good news over and over again.

"But my *eyes!*"

I was sure my eyes would nix it.

"Hazel, am I right?"

"That's what I *mean!*"

I'd always meant to take a few lessons. Just never got around to it.

"Hey, what can I tell ya? It was neck an' neck wit' you an' Tom Crowfoot, whose mudda came over in a teepee, for chrissake. They went *anudda way*, that's all. Say good-bye."

"Good-bye."

"Good-bye."

Whoever heard of Crisscross Productions?

HER NAME WAS Nancy and it was love at first sight. Ordinarily demure, she rubbed her smallish forehead on my chest the day we met. She was either brown with white spots or white with brown spots—one never knew, for it depended on the whim of the sun—and lived at

Pickwick Stables on the outskirts of Burbank with Carlo, the stable boy who was also smallish. Nancy was a pinto. If I'm not mistaken, Tonto had a pinto.

For two weeks I gripped her, albeit gently, with my thighs as man and beast drifted aimlessly together as one, above the din of the freeway, through the rolling trails—so designated—of Burbank, overlooking sleepy Glendale. Nancy always knew when the hour was up, and that's smart. Then we'd have a little canter.

I never had a pet of my very own because Ev is allergic; however, I don't believe I've inherited that tendency. Maybe a little. What a chuckle. If I could have my druthers, I'd hitch up old Nancy to the back of the Alfa and take her home in a trot and give her lots of carrots and sugar and a big hug every night.

"TO SEGURO, son of the chief, and his stallion, Nancy." Jay lifted his daiquiri with a smirk. "And get yourself some Nair, baby."

"Nair, *baby?*"

"Nair, *baby,*" repeated Jay, a little hurt, I think, because he thought I was mimicking him. "When's the last time you saw a full-blooded Apache with hair on his chest?"

I was at a loss.

"Or arms and legs for that matter?"

"I guess you're right."

"Of course I'm right."

"What are you having?" I asked.

"If you'll notice, I'm perusing the menu as we speak."

"I'm sorry."

"You're such a wise-ass sometimes."

"I don't mean to be. How 'bout the chiffonade salad," I suggested. "You like that."

"I'm fed up with the chiffonade. You are, you know you are."

"You started it."

"John fucking-Wayne."

"I'm not."

"All rolled into one."

"Bullshit." I gave it some thought. "Often?"

"Three days before you set foot on an airplane."

"How 'bout the broiled chicken?"

"It's called whistling in the dark. I'm having the sauerbrauten—it's on special. And get yourself some fucking Nair."

I MADE SURE my seat back was in its upright position, fastened my seat belt, secured my tray table, and visualized myself stark naked, standing majestically on the tippy-top of the highest peak in the universe, feet firmly rooted to Mother Earth while every other fiber of my being stretched upward, onward, and outward into a pink firmament of airy bliss. It works for Jay, it works for me, I decided, as Western Airlines Flight 502 made it.

A week in Mexico would do all of me a world of good.

I T W A S ten A.M. and already hot at the smallish Guaymas Aeropuerto (it says here), equipped with a shack. How on earth did we find it? And sure to get hotter, I thought, as three Charles Bronsons patted down my luggage while their pets looked on, and I browsed the area for a connecting flight to a place called Creel (it says here). Sounds like a fish nobody ever heard of.

And I spotted her.

She was outside, not twenty feet away, propped on a suitcase.

From inside out, I spotted her.

Upon a stylish suitcase she lounged on the little runway, chin in hand, face away, staring off into near space, it appeared, at one of those miniature-type airplanes that one expects to see dangling helplessly from the ceiling of an airport bar—except this little devil was not a true miniature. It had obviously held people at one time in its career.

I made my way out of the shack and moved softly toward her and allowed her back to reveal itself to me in a series of shots. Faded blue Levi's. Sneakers. No socks. Ankles. Chopped hair that barely gave a damn. A hundred-year-old chambray shirt. Tied at the waist? I wondered.

I toyed with and eventually formulated a clever arrival

at her side, when she turned on me. Swiveled as in molasses and remained so lovely as a bent crane.

"Buenos días, Johnny B.," said Claire Fairchild Van Horn.

Only in Hollywood, I thought.

xxiv
• • •

"**S**ee?" I explained to Margie. "The idea being, Charlton Heston isn't exactly—you know—your world beater. For instance, Brando he ain't, or a Clift or a . . . see, that's the punch line. That's what makes it funny. Because he's been so goddamn *lucky*."

"I get it."

"Good. How 'bout one for the road?"

"Hell, might as well be drunk as the way I am."

Jerry saw me coming from behind the bar, for the atmosphere had dwindled some. Dazzle for the most part had called it a night, and one was aware that the room was indeed painted black. By now everybody knew exactly what the wee hours had in store.

We sat for a spell.

I plucked at the perimeter of yet another cocktail napkin under my glass, little by little around its edges in order to form a perfect circle underneath. It's an octagon, stupid.

She fumbled in her purse for a fresh pack of cigarettes, opened them, and lit one before I could get to my lighter.

It had all been said, and all in all it had been a helluva night. Margie Cosgrove. It's good to go back. What kind of a woman might she have become, say, if Beryl had shipped her ass off to Bennington instead of—

"You know what he was lucky in?"

I feared the worst. "Who?"

"Charlton Heston."

"No."

"That Western."

"Which?"

"*Will* something."

"*Penny.*"

"Yeah."

"*Will Penny.*"

"That's the one."

"With Joan Hackett."

"Who?"

"It doesn't matter. You're right."

"Wasn't he terrific?"

"Pretty terrific."

God, I was exhausted.

"God," she said, "you used to tell the best jokes."

I excused myself, made my way the length of Ports and into the john, which was vacant, and attempted unsuccessfully to make the bubbles extend to the entire inner circumference of the bowl. Keep the child, Phoebe used to say.

"Speaking of Westerns," Margie added immediately on my return, "I saw you last week."

"No."

"The hell I didn't. In an old movie. Something *Arrow*."

"*Wobbly*," I suggested.

"*Poised Arrow*—that's it. Boy, did you ever look gorgeous on that horse."

"I did?"

"And all those muscles! Man, you were meaner 'n hell."

"I was?"

"Anyway, that's what did it."

"Did what?"

"Made me call you, finally."

"That's what did it?"

She began with a pause during which she took a long drag from her Marlboro, blew smoke in a thin stream up and away, and dismissed with a wave of the hand the residue from the distance between us. Straight at me: "You should have played the lead." Then beyond me: "I don't know how come you don't have your own series or something." Briefly to the wall: "Anyway, Harley snores like a buffalo, so I went in the living room and turned on the tube." Back at me: "And there you were."

This chick really knows how to play a monologue.

To her glass: "All those muscles and how electric you were. I'll never forget the day we met and I took one look ..." right between the eyes: "... at that gorgeous body and all that beautiful hair—it looks neat gray, by the way—and thought: oh, shit, I've found my man."

"How long are you staying in L.A.?"

She took an age to crush her cigarette. "Boy, we sure came close that night. Almost but not quite," she crushed, poetically. "I'll never forget the look on your face that last night when I walked out of your car. You looked like somebody'd just slapped the shit outta you. I just turned around and walked away and started crying." Face-to-face: "How long am I staying in Los Angeles?"

"Yeah."

"Just tonight." A tear formed and hung. "Anyway, that's what made me start crying—the look on your face."

"Oh, jeez."

"At my girlfriend's where you picked me up."

"In Inglewood."

"That's it, Inglewood. It's kind of a . . ."

"Nice—"

". . . ratty neighborhood, mostly your Hispanics, but it's nice inside."

"Yes."

"My girlfriend, Geneva, she's in Las Vegas . . ."

"You said."

"Just so I feed the dog in the morning."

"By gad, sir, you *are* a character, that you are."

The Maltese Falcon
WARNER BROS., 1941

XXV

• • •

"**W**hat a terrific coincidence!" trilled Claire, literally through rose-colored glasses, big, round, and smoky, as SEGURO, flamboyant son of the chief, and HATTIE, stoic daughter of the plains (it says here on page forty-two) sat side by side on suitcases at the aeropuerto in far-off Mexico. She smiled at the sky, and the top half of her had a good stretch. The hundred-year-old chambray shirt was indeed tied loosely above the waist. A thin line of what I would imagine to be the finest down imaginable made its way from below her navel devil-may-care into her jeans, which were button-fly. The aroma was Jean Naté after-bath. "We can go horseback riding!"

"What kind of an airplane would you call *that?*" I asked, masking a vivid interest with a crooked grin.

"Quaint," decided Claire, and she went on to explain in some detail that quaint ones have the ability to glide if necessary.

That's when I saw them.

On the tail of her story they came, two short men, hazy out of the horizon of my astigmatism and onto the runway. In the two-shot of my mind I cut to Gable and Tracy, a-goggle, a-grin, arm in arm, and danced them into the cockpit of my heart . . .

They wore baseball caps the funny way, bent cigarettes hung from two mouths that were dead, and they weaved in our general direction.

The stoic waved her ass off.

And dirty shirts (God knows what), and they scratched and they picked and they rubbed and they poked, and as far as I could surmise rooted to my Samsonite, they were trying to remember what a fucking wing looks like. I'm sorry, Jesus, but Christ!

" I HAVE this lavish feeling," said Claire in a reverie, "that I could simply reach down and brush the treetops." Ponderosa pines by the thousands, she'd informed me on takeoff. "What a pity you can't open the eisinglass without opening the door."

Wilbur and Orville lounged up front and we scrunched up back.

I wanted us all to be good friends.

"Buenas días," I stated.

"Buen*os* días," she corrected. "Días es masculino and takes the *o*."

"Oh." Live-in help, I thought.

"That's it. I don't think they heard you."

"How long is this flight, I wonder."

"Quanto tiempo à Creel?" she blared.

"No sé. Hora y media. Mas o menos."

"Hour and a half, am I right?"

"Very good," smiled Claire, as if I'd just graduated third grade with honors.

But we're not a hundred-and-ten percent certain.

Are we? I said to myself.

He shrugged. I saw him shrug.

Both pilot and copilot actually had a pretty good shrug, and the one on the left scratched his head.

I saw him.

She peeled a Baby Ruth, dropped the wrapper on her lap, and offered me first bite, which I took. Before I could thank her eye-to-eye, she withdrew a *New Yorker* from her Louis Vuitton carryall and disappeared into a hot/cool world about which I was curious.

I committed to memory the time of the day and set up a vigil of sorts, eventually moved it from my Timex to the back of *The Head of Alfredo Garcia* . . .

To the gasolina gauge . . .

To the ear of the guy on my right.

I clutched my Naugahyde and made love to the trees.

To the fur on the back of her neck, for she'd fallen asleep. It's a beautiful day. Everything will be fine.

And chewed some gum and listened for sounds and counted the E's on the sports page of the *Los Angeles Times.*

"Claire?" I nudged her pretty shoulder gently. "Claire?"

"Mmm."

"Time is up. Has been up for a little while, and our crew seems to be hunched over a matchbook cover," I added good-naturedly. "And one guy shakes his head sí and the other guy shakes his head no—and look at that: they're pointing in different directions. Nine different directions. What a trip! You think you could ask them? Stan and Ollie? Whooooopsie-daisy . . . I like it when they bank like that and make circles . . . I believe we're descending . . . Whooops, wrong again. Does it concern you in the slightest that the gasolina is . . . we *are* descending. *Good job missing that* . . . Is on *E*? The gasolina? Whooooops . . ."

"Yes."

"Yes?"

"Of course."

Soon we were holding hands.

Hard.

The sleep twins climbed languidly toward the fingertip of God, much the way Rosalind Russell committed suicide in *Flight for Freedom.*

As if revived by lack of oxygen, they came to quiet rapproachement, *mas o menos*, and pointed accidentally in the same direction at the same moment, give or take, acknowledging a flat place the size of a manhole cover, and went for it.

And presently the little airship that could—how like a

movie, I thought—banged right side up and whacked every chink, rock, and dimple south of Pico and Sepulveda before it eventually coughed, wheezed, and humped to a conclusive halt before hitting the base of a mountain. Bueno, it's dead.

How like a movie.

CAMERA PANS a good 360 to REVEAL nothing.
WE HEAR a prehistoric breeze whisper from pine top to pine top, signifying nothing.
WE SEE her move off, as if to find something.

                    HE
            (to them in their lingo)
        Is Creel?

                    THEY
            (to him in his)
        I think so.

He moves to her.

FULL SHOT.

                    SHE
            (to no one)
        The Sierra Madre mountain range is 2000
        miles long and 100 miles wide and is composed
        of canyons and volcanic material that make it a
        bitch to cross. Did you know that?
                    HE
        We're lost.

> SHE
> (off his look)

I know.

MEDIUM SHOT.

She removes a compact from her Louis Vuitton, checks the mirror, brushes a speck from an eyelash, and freshens her lipstick.

How like the movies.

That even as we are on the edge of our seats, the camera whips a 180 to reveal a roar and a ball of dust that turns into a truck, a cousin of our plane. It appears, but faster, in a dead heat in our direction. We see that sucker stop on a peso directly in front of us, forming a nice group shot of the gang that hacked everybody in *Treasure of the Sierra Madre*, with half a dozen children in tow who seem hardly old enough to carry rifles.

> HE
> (with song in his heart)

Buenos días!

TWO SHOT. INT. cab of truck. THE LOPEZ BROTHERS. SINGLE. Her.

> SHE
> (singularly)

Estamos aquí para estudiar los artifactos de los Indios Tarahumara. No hay gasolina en nuestro avion y estamos perdidos. Creel es lejos? Cual es el mejor manera de ir a Creel de aquí?

WE WIDEN TO INCLUDE:

The back of the flatbed, children sullen, deprived, armed.

SHE

*Tengo un presente para esta niña linda. Posso a
presentarle à ella?*

She moves to the flatbed, digs into her Louis, and hands
over the compact to the saddest little girl, the barest and
sparest, and while the women chat on about how to open it
and use it and see the pretty faces, we . . .

CUT TO:

Them huddling with them.

INSERT: gasolina into aeroplano.

DISSOLVE TO:

The little truck roaring out of existence, kicking up such a
flurry of dust we barely make out a glint of sunshine playing on a fading compact, waving adiós from the tailgate
and disappearing south of the border down Mexico way.

INTERCUT CLOSE-UPS.

Look at him.

Look at her.

How like the El Rey.

SHE LICKED thick salt from the top of her lean right
hand.
   "Imagine," she said.
   "What?" I asked, licking mine.
   She knocked back a tequila.

"Did you know we're eight thousand feet above Dupar's?"

I followed suit.

"I knew we were high."

She sucked lemon and so did I.

It was near closing time at the barrito in the small Motel Parador de la Montaña in the little town of Creel, population six hundred. Juanito plucked absently in the near corner.

She rested her chin in the palms of her hands and ate the table with her body. "Did you know that only six hundred people live here?"

I sat back and liked it. "We almost hit the sign pulling into town."

"Did you know that?"

"One could almost reach down and brush it . . ."

"You're a good listener . . ."

". . . with his fingertips."

"Did you know that a couple of years ago, I said to myself, is he ready for me?"

"No."

"Yet?"

"Yes?"

"Sí. Did you know that?"

She eased a hand on my knee.

I felt it on my heart.

She made a move to remove her rose-colored glasses.

"Leave them on," I suggested.

"Mas tarde," she whispered.

Which means

Later.

xxvi
• • •

"Hi," I ventured softly as I stood next to his head, which was the size and color of a locomotive, and sipped coffee from a plastic cup. He heard me.

He chose to ignore.

The wrangler, a real Marlboro Man, had introduced me to my horse by kicking his ass, dragging him toward me, and handing me the reins. Whereupon he deserted us for a fried egg sandwich with bacon, cheese, tomato, and onion—a filmdom tradition in the A.M.—and left us alone to establish rapport.

What the hell. I'll eat tomorrow.

The night had had a thousand eyes, the scenery was breathtaking, the morning delightful—I had a need to share my joy, so I tried to touch his mane.

"I baptize thee, Nancy." I chuckled. "I have a little problem with Sumbitch," I confided.

He flicked.

"But what's in a name?" I soothed.

He indicated his tree trunk of a neck my way and took the carrot. "You look ridiculous," he said with savage wisdom.

Which was untrue.

I felt ridiculous, and I never looked better in my life. Mirror-mirror in makeup told me so.

"It's the wig," I whispered. "They made little teepees out of Seguro's existing hair," I explained, "and skewered it in some cases to the bone."

He pretended to be otherwise involved.

"It hurts when I breathe."

Sumbitch jerked away in disgust. "You look like Velveeta."

"It's the Nair, baby."

"Velveeta with a fringe on top."

"Horses can't talk."

"Take my word."

SON OF THE CHIEF and daughter of the plains, however, rarely spoke to one another on the set and never had breakfast together. Befitting a relationship between cowgirls and Indians, explained Claire. Hiding at night from the cast and the crew was adventuresome enough, we agreed. For a pal of her pal was producing this thing. And a friend of a friend had invested. Maybe a toe touch once in a while at lunch.

THE LENGTH and breadth and vastness of Copper Canyon, for which Creel is famous—with its cascading waterfalls, awesome and magnificent and unique—can only be fully experienced from the rim of disaster.

"I'm in love."

"I'm not interested in your personal life."

" *'Choo!* Ow."

"Gesundheit."

"Thank you." I wanted to pat his head—he likes it when I do—but I didn't care to make the lean. "Aren't we standing a little close to the edge?"

"I like it on the edge," confessed Sumbitch.

"Could . . . could we just move over just a little? Please? *Not that way!*"

"*Now* we're on the edge."

I TOLD HER I love you when she wasn't looking, and she poked her head out of the bathroom as if in surprise and smiled all over and sighed the most wonderful sigh.

No one looks like so

In a terrycloth robe

Mid-thigh.

Memorize her from across the room.

No one moves like so

From shower

To bed

With hair

Not quite dry.

Memorize her like so.

She opened her mouth and bit at my cheeks and tickled the back of my neck and put her mouth around my mouth and sucked me till my scalp itched and I asked no questions.

No one

Touches

Or tastes

Or gives

Or takes

Like so.

Memorize her.

She pushed me back on the bed and sat on my thighs and flirted with us till some crazy people came along and took us away.

Which is she

Which is me

One can't tell

From the smell

Of us all.

Don't try.

"*PLEASE,*" I begged into Sumbitch's big black ear. No thanks to gravity, Seguro was close enough to eat it as he groped for handles and clung for life and his wig ran away up his nose.

"*Please*

    slow

        down."

"Your braves are gaining on you."

"*I*

    don't

        care."

"You want to be the last asshole at the wagon train?"

"*Y*

  e

    s."

"I can fix that."

"*No!*

  Watch

    that

      tree."

"Gesundheit. Which tree?"

"THAT ONE!

    You

      cocksucker."

"Hey!"

"*W*

  h

    a

      t?"

"Aren't you supposed to say something courageous? After all, we are in frame."

"Yaaaaaaaaaahhhhh ...!"
"Very nice."

CLAIRE FOUND an old woman
  Who lived in a shack
  A shack at the far end of town.
  Claire found an old woman
  With a hump on her back
  Who lived in a shack
  With a pig in the back
  At the far end of town.
  Who cooked
      And who looked
          And who smiled
              While we dined
                  Holding hands.
  "Ya-da-ya-da, Warden."
  "Never mind those Louis Armstrong impressions," she
answered, passing the salsa.

CUT TO:

The close-up.

One's signature shot.

  Seguro is required to be menacing and stock-still on
his mount lest he lean out of frame, for his face fills the
silver screen and is two to three stories high, depending
on the size of the theatre. Fans may jump into a pore if

they so desire. The smart actor saves his best stuff for the magical close-up. In this case: "Me see white man!" By comparison, a wide shot of the red man hurtling through trees and whipping past the lens into a Conestoga wagon is but a blur on the screen. Similarly, sitting atop a thousand-pound bully on a faraway cliff, facing the camera on one side and certain death on the other, becomes insignificant to the mature audience if the scenery is breathtaking.

"You're rationalizing," said Sumbitch.

I paid him no mind. "Look, we've had our fun, have we not?" I murmured to his belly under my breath and through my teeth as I leaned down from his back, and Makeup covered my scratches and Hair pulled hair from my nose. I was not about to dismount and remount. He doesn't like it when I do. I straightened. "We need to be verrry still now," I added, gently patting his mane. "You prick."

"I heard that."

"Sorry.

"Sorry's not enough."

I continued to ignore him to the best of my ability.

Who am I? I asked myself.

"You're a lovesick wuss," answered Sumbitch.

I am Seguro, son of the chief.

"Action!" yelled the director, whose name was Frank.

"Stop me if you've seen this one," whispered Sumbitch.

"Getting to knowww you . . ." Step, two, three . . .

"Cut!"

"Or dance along if you like."

"Action!"

"Getting to knowww all about you . . ." Step, four . . .

"Cut!"

And the melody lingered on. For nine takes. Till the cinematographer, whose name was Alex and who'd been crippled by vicious bowel activity for two weeks, allowed as how he didn't make the trip to this godforsaken place just to shit and shoot half an Apache. While he was in the john, the assistant director, Ronnie, whose job it is to save time and money, summoned four wranglers, each of whom hunkered below the lens and grabbed a leg and rooted that Sumbitch to the ground.

"Action!"

"Me see white man!"

"Cut, print."

Seguro dismounted forever. He thought better of kicking his noble steed in an area that would give him the ultimate dancing lesson. Instead he promised himself if he ever saw Burbank again, he'd hitch up sweet Nancy to the back of the Alfa, drive her to the amusement park on the Santa Monica pier, and nail her hooves to the merry-go-round where she belongs.

xxvii
· · ·

Leave it to Rusty. He loves talking to little old ladies in Monrovia and other small communities to the east. And they love talking to him, which is why he's making a small fortune. "Mother, dear, you just make your way into the kitchen right this minute. Do you hear me . . . ?" And before he can explain the ins and outs of the policy, which he confesses he doesn't even understand completely as God is his witness, Mother toodles off to the coffee can. Once in a while he even gets a macaroon.

Which is good.

For Rusty.

Because, and he's the first to admit it, there's a whole bunch more Jimmy Cagney inside his head when he's knocking some mizzable prick twice his size on his ass at Tom Bergin's Irish pub on Fairfax than there ever was on the silver screen. "So help me, champ!"

I like working for Jake.

One, you don't have to think a lot.

Two, it's not steady.

Three, he pays under the table.

Four, loading and unloading dressers and sofas and headboards is a hell of a way to stay in shape and I can still collect unemployment.

Jake says he loves actors because they have bullshit that won't quit.

Obviously, I can't afford a steady job.

I see here in the newsletter from Screen Actors Guild that we may be going on strike, and Stan says that business has never been so bad.

Rusty keeps urging me to jump on the phone with his girlfriend. Leave it to Rusty.

Other mail.

Phoenix, Arizona

Dear Mr. Bruno,

May I tell you what definite pleasure you give me when I see you on television? I have always been your most ardent fan and it is such a joy to sit at your feet and watch your incredibly simple and selective performances. Thank you for having touched my life. I know that due to your busy schedule you have little spare time and also that you have thousands of admirers, but could you find a moment to have your secretary send me an autographed picture of yourself, you would make me the happiest person in the world and I would frame it and keep it for ever and ever.

> Your most ardent fan,
> Staci

P.S. Here is a snapshot of me.
P.P.S. I am thinner now.

I will file that.

I will send Staci a glossy with an appropriate message neatly written on the lower left-hand corner and file that letter in my box, in the blue folder marked PERSONAL.

Ev used to say, "Bruno Sangenito, you eat your dinner around and around. Never mind saving the best part for last!" Which in this case is a picture postcard with a lavish photo of the Empire State Building, where Cary Grant waited his ass off for Deborah Kerr in *An Affair to Remember*.

NYC

Johnny B.
Arr. Pan Am 1217, 10:30 P.M. on third.

Jeans, I think.

And a sweater. My yellow sweater with the V-neck and my peace sign and sneakers would be good.

And leave the apartment early because these things take a little time to plan. Plenty of notepaper. Two pens just in case. And don't be a schmuck, get gas on the way and check the slow leak in the right rear. She'll be blown away. And pray for a small crowd at the airport. Just enough to keep it safe and make it fun.

There was a medium to small crowd at LAX and it was still early, so I browsed Gate 37 and its environs, all but ignoring the sweet brunette who smiled back at me from behind the counter. I tried to imagine what she'd be wearing off the plane, then I settled down in the coffee shop and went to work. Luckily I brought two pens, although the waitress had a red that I liked, and I settled on it.

Scotch tape!

Shit fuck, I forgot the Scotch tape.

I must say, Hazel was very nice about it even though she was working two stations because somebody didn't show. So I said, "Not now necessarily because I'm not sure what I want to say yet. Let me just figure it out first because if I've only got one strip of tape to deal with, I better get it right the first time." She agreed.

Ten-fifteen P.M. FLT. 1217—ON TIME, it said under arrivals.

I rested the tape lightly on my big knuckle and folded the paper back and forth and back and forth and ran thumb and forefinger down its crease in order to create a perfect tear, for it needed to be large enough to be conspicuous to the conscious and small enough to be inconspicuous to the unconscious.

Her word, not mine.

Ten twenty P.M. FLT. 1217—LANDED.

Early.

I placed it in the palm of my left hand, since that's my stronger side, and made myself small and inconspicuous—I should have been a spy. I moved casually toward the down escalator leading to baggage claim. The ceiling drops in a giant right angle to conform to the descent.

. . . Four, three, two, one, whack!

It stuck. I turned to see if it had fallen, and it had stuck.

I made a quick U-turn, for the up escalator is adjacent to the down and at one point during its ascent crosses the plane of the right angle that juts from the ceiling, and one could almost reach out and touch it.

Ten twenty-five P.M. I became *A Face in the Crowd*.

And waited.

It's funny about waiting.

And played "What do you know, she smiled at me in my dreams last night" with the tip of my tongue against the inside of my lower teeth.

And waited.

. . . Four, three, two, one . . .

He wore a necktie.

Give me a break.

Five hours from N.Y. to L.A., first-class or no first-class, and *The Putz in the Iron Mask* wears a tie and one of his thirty-seven cashmere sport jackets. And pressed slacks. How do you work that one out? Just lucky, I guess. And a pink shirt?

Give me a break.

She wore New Yorkie–baggy blue jeans, of course, and sturdy walking shoes because she loves to do Manhattan while he's being a cowboy—"A surgeon is a cowboy who cuts and slashes and moves on." If I've heard it once . . . She also wore the salt-and-pepper shaggy-dog coat we made love under at *High Noon* in her backseat in who knows whose carport. She was walking a little behind him and chatted away at the back of his gray head as if to make him feel at home as they moved apace toward the down escalator.

. . . Four, three, two, one . . .

She saw it!

I know she saw it. I saw her see it: the perfect arrow, poised and well-drawn. She looked all around and she saw me, which means *mas tarde*, I'm pretty sure she saw me in the crowd, throwing pebbles at the window of her mind.

xxviii

• • •

I am so right for a love story it isn't even funny. And I told as much to Stan even though he'd made the call to me and I'd barely given him a chance to say good morning. To fall asleep at night dodging bullets and to be awakened at ten A.M. by a summons from one's artist representative while holding hands with a happy ending is what it's all about.

"Yeah? Well hold the thought. This here audition on which I am sending you is something for which you are on the schnozzola. We're not talkin' your run'a da mill TV heavy here. No silk stockin' over da face, no ski mask. How many times I gotta live that one down? Who knows from wardrobe? We're talkin' here, and mark my woids, maybe da best fuckin' *major* . . . motion . . . picture in years ta come. Could win ten Oscars before they cast it awreddy—an' loaded wit' high-class gangsters. We're talkin' here the mafiosos."

"No kidding."

"Your people."

"No kidding."

"Paramount, three o'clock tomorra with Francis Ford Coppola no less. Later you'll do *Romeo and Juliet*."

I WAS almost giggling. It was five-thirty and there wasn't much of a dinner crowd at the Nickodell, which is walking distance from Paramount. Counting steps was out of the question, for it was difficult to contain myself under the circumstances. I'd called Claire first, from a pay phone on the lot—and she was thrilled. Then Stan. God knows I'd been wanting to buy him a nice dinner for some time now because he's been so steadfast, and here was the perfect opportunity. "First of all," I said, "I told him my real name, which I don't think hurt at all." I could hardly wait for the waiter to drop everything and leave us the hell alone.

Even Stan was almost giggling. "So tell me."

I took a deep breath. "Anyway, I had to wait forever because everybody in town was there. Which was good in a sense, for the business, I mean."

"Casta thousands."

"Anybody with an iota of Italian blood."

"Nu?"*

"Which was also good because I had an hour or so to go over the scene in the hall. So finally I go in. And I'm

So what else is nu?

not nervous. I mean, I feel at home, and Coppola was terrific. I even called him Francis. I took the chance— that's how relaxed I was."

"You should always be relaxed. Look at me."

"Right, so anyway, I was telling him about where I was born and raised and stuff, and you know what he asked me?"

"I should know what he asked you?"

I sat back. Awash with gaiety. "How come Jews always answer a question with a question?"

"Why shouldn't a Jew answer a question wit' a question?"

I leaned in. "Who did *I* think should play the lead! He actually asked *me* who should play the lead in *The Godfather*!"

"Who'd ja go wit?"

"Brando."

"Good choice."

"Anyway, then he brought this other actor in—I forget his name—and asked him a bunch of questions and then we played the scene, the two of us. And he thanked the other guy and he looked right at me and asked me to stick around! Then he actually had another actor come in and he has me read the scene with him!"

"No."

"How often does *that* happen? Anyway, we read the scene—and you know how it gets better the second time around. Anyway, we read the scene and he thanks the other guy and everybody sort of looks around and thanks everybody else and I get up to leave and he asks me to stick around *again*!"

"No."

"Emmis! And here's the clincher!"

"Have some shrimp."

"This girl comes in, this actress, medium attractive, and he gets up from his desk, shakes her hand and tells her to sit in his seat."

"Behind da desk."

"Exactly. And he walks to the other end of the office just opposite her and he turns on this little camera."

"On her."

"Yeah. And by now I'm right at home, and Mr. Coppola turns on the camera and without so much as a glance my way says, 'Ask her some questions, Johnny!' "

"No."

"Yeah! And you know what?"

"Tell me."

"I gave him my very best Phoebe Sax."

"This is good?"

"You tell me: is there any way Johnny Bruno is not going to be in *The Godfather*?"

I COULDN'T BELIEVE my ears.

"You're kidding."

"Would I kid?"

"But I had it."

"What can I say?"

"He loved me."

"It's a freaky business."

"I guess."

"No rules."

"I guess."

"No logic."

"I guess."

"They went anudda way, that's all."

IT'S ONLY a ten-minute drive from the Van Horn household in Malibu, south on Pacific Coast Highway to the Lindomar Motel at the foot of Sunset, especially at nine-thirty A.M. when those who drive into town to business are on their way and the community is quiet. We only do it when we can't resist, and Claire's never late.

This morning she was late.

As usual she wore her bulky purple and beige broad-striped floor-to-ceiling bathrobe with the hood on top, and poured black coffee from the home pot into a pair of decorative rough-surfaced cups from her kitchen shelf. I took them to be ours. Mine is turquoise with orange circles. As usual she wore no makeup and smelled of Jean Naté and toothpaste. We sat sipping on the bed as usual. When Claire said we have to stop. She placed her decorative cup on the floor next to mine, and before I could dream of untying a shoe, she laid the palm of her hand onto the back of mine, much the way she eased it onto my knee when we had to start, and looked at me and said we have to stop now. And begged me not to one-ring her anymore, which is our secret night signal to each other that one of us is thinking about the other. Stop now, and I tried not to be a sissy. She never once fooled with her glasses or touched my face. She's very strong, a wonderful quality in a woman, and I tried not to be such a sissy. We held hands then, hard for a moment like we did on the little airplane for a moment. She felt so adored, she said, so adored, and it was extraordinary, Johnny B., and she's never felt so adored. She kissed my fingers good-bye and I tried to say we'll always have Aspen, something fractured, because she has such a quirky sense of humor.

She got pregnant
One night in Bermuda
Thinking of me
And went another way.

Phoenix, Arizona

Dear Johnny Bruno,
I can't thank you enough for the wonderful picture of yourself. I hate to be a pest, but if you happen to have one with your shirt off or something, I can't believe I'm being such a *pest*!

Devotedly,
Staci

It's best not to think too much about Crisco.
"Crisp, not greasy!"
"Uh, that's fine," said one of the four young faces

from across the room and behind the desk. Three man-faces, one woman-face—all graduates of stern school. "Now . . . would you do it for us again, and pretend you've got a piece of chicken in your hand while you say the line?"

"Sure thing." I waved the invisible chicken, I chose a drumstick. "Mmmmm, crisp. Not greasy!"

Phoebe says commercials have nothing to do with acting.

"Better. Nice. Uh . . . now try it again and lose the *mmmmm* and hit the crisp."

"You bet," I said from experience, and I really hit it. "*Crisp*. Not greasy!"

Everybody looked at everybody. "Okay . . . nice . . . nice," said the spokes-face. "Now try it and glance at the chicken in your hand on *crisp* and then a big smile at your wife and a wink at the kids."

I was alone on my side of the desk, is the reason I felt so alone. I took a moment to calculate. Lose *mmmmm*, hit *crisp*, glance chicken, smile wife, wink kids, I thought.

Somebody across the desk leaned toward his or her neighbor and whispered something secret. "Oh, and don't wave the chicken. Just hold the chicken."

"Right you are." Don't wave, lose *mmmmm*, hit *crisp*, glance chicken, smile wife . . .

"And see if you can't cut two seconds off the time."

. . . wink kids and make it snappy.

There is not an acting teacher in the world that is right about everything.

"Crisp!" I made what I thought to be a fairly interesting commitment to the concept, but quickly as I glanced at the air between my fingers—which by now had become a big fat brown sizzly piece of farm-fresh chicken straight from the frying pan. *"Not* greasy!" I gave it a little extra just for dash and smiled warmly at the telephone at the far end of the desk, where I had straddled Donna Reed and winked at our two happy hungry tots, forks poised, on the rim of the ashtray, near the corner.

"Thank you."

"Thank *you!"* I answered, hitting the you, I'm sure from force of habit. I couldn't help noticing that for the first time since I'd walked into the room nice-casual they all smiled at me from across the desk nice-very, as in life-still.

"On the nose."

"I'm pleased . . ."

"Absolutely on the nose."

". . . that you're pleased."

"With a second to spare. Are you available . . ."

"We so seldom . . ."

". . . next Thursday?"

". . . get feedback. I beg your pardon?"

"Are you available next Thursday?"

"That would be . . ."

"The sixteenth."

"As far as I know." One must always hedge on future availability—true Hollywood legend—for what if the impossible slips between the cracks in the interim? "As far as I know," I repeated thoughtfully, and made my gracious exit with the utmost confidence in my availability. Screw the Mafia.

What a neat idea, I thought as I left the lobby of the Château Marmont on Sunset, where New York people love to stay when they're casting. Sleep in one room and audition in another. Screw Claire, too. I wondered about their parties at the Château, and maybe I'll get invited up after the shoot. She watches very little television, only the good shows. But Crisco is a national spot—and one night when she's all alone in the den in damp Malibu with her head in her hands, bored stiff and can't sleep because she's flooded with memories . . . I thought as I hung a left on La Cienega, maybe the guy who got my part in *The Godfather* will have a heart attack. I wonder who they'll get to play my wife and kids. First I'll get new tires and spruce up the Alfa . . .

Phoenix, Arizona

Dear Johnny,

    I absolutely adore my picture, Mr. Tarzan! I mean I *adore* it, and if you ever feel tempted to talk to a really true-blue fan you just dial (602) 949–7341 nights only. Ha, ha.

Yours,
Staci

I couldn't believe my ears.

"You're kidding."

"Ya didn't *lose* the part. Somebody else *got* the part, is all."

"But I had it."

"What can I say?"

"They loved me."

"It's a freaky business."

"I know."

"No rules."

"I know."

"No logic."

"I know."

"They went—"

"Another way, I know."

"That's all."

"Which way this time?"

"Paul Mantee."

No rules, I concluded.

" PHOENIX must be beautiful this time of year," I said into the phone that night, and she couldn't believe her ears.

xxix

• • •

A tree. Let's do a tree. Let's go with a tree in winter.

MONTAGE DISSOLVE—TIME SEQUENCE

    A) WE SEE the who am I tree, its bare limbs
        shiver in the cruel winter snow.
    B) Spring now: leaves in evidence.
        No buds, just leaves.
    C) Autumn now: leaves wither, drop, and
        glide. They have the ability to glide toward
        the windswept earth.
    D) Winter again . . .

Leave us not go overboard, Aunt Rose would say.

I neglected even to mention the project at hand to Ev because nobody will see dis picture, as Stan would have said.

Although it's hardly pornographic.

His passing was painless, Ramona says. He fell into his short ribs at the Cock 'n' Bull an' went out wit' a smile, he would have said.

Pornography is not allowed on television, by definition.

The service was in Hebrew.

Nu?

And I hung on to my yarmulke.

The Ashley-Taylor Artists Group, Ltd., a prestige outfit indeed, occupies the entire eleventh floor of the 9000 Building on upper Sunset, and although it's difficult to have a heart-to-heart with one of the many many agents who form the company—ATAG is loaded with protective secretaries—they are, it turns out, aware of my work.

They'll never see my cock.

In *Love Ya, Nurse Jane.*

They assured me.

And not much of Cindy-Mindy Merriweather, either, I would imagine, save a breast or two here and there. Can't imagine for the life of me how one could possibly photograph a teleplay about a sex surrogate who saves a dozen marriages on a special channel without some, partial, a little . . .

Just my legs probably.

My ankles and my knees and my thighs. And my back, chest, arms, and face probably.

Mostly Cindy-Mindy.

Imagine a teleplay without a face.

IT WORKED.

Nurse Jane wore a camisole, black.

Her patient stood by the raging fire in nurse's rustic living room, soaked to his skin, dressy-sport. Outside, driving rain pelted the known world relentlessly.

Soon they were naked.

The patient, seemingly unsure for a moment despite three rehearsals in a kimono, eventually lay on his back on the carpet at her bidding, and the camera followed Nurse Jane as she melted down and sat on the middle of him.

With a pickle in the middle and the mustard on top, he thought, which is why it began to work.

. . . *Just the way you like it and they're all red hot* . . . he sang to himself.

Which made him chuckle, which is why it worked.

Ultimately.

For even though the patient was in relative discomfort, smashed as he was against the inside of his own left thigh, he began to move, jerkily, rhythmically, involuntarily upward and downward as befits a muffled chuckle. Which Nurse Jane translated as a commitment to therapy. And pinned as he was, he couldn't help staring up between what appeared to be Cindy and Mindy and beyond at the ceiling of a soundstage on the lot of historic

Columbia Pictures, where visions of Burt Lancaster and that group vanished as he chose to go with Jack Benny. And Nurse Jane sighed, "Oh, baby." Presently, when the pigeons in the rafters, who've lived there forever and seen it all, began to coo, the patient took it as boo and could hardly contain himself, and Nurse Jane went berserk.

XXX

• • •

I am so right for a love story it isn't even funny. And I told as much to Dr. Krym. I have no idea how he felt about that awareness on my part or even if he heard me because I'm not allowed to look. I'm allowed to lie there and count the little holes in the acoustical ceiling and reach in back of me for a Kleenex if necessary. Apparently, it's also against the rules to ask a question. Last week on entering the office I merely inquired, "How are you, Dr. Krym?" And he pointed to the brown couch and said, "Nevah mind how am *I*. How ah *you*?"

So?

Where does one go with that piece of news?

"Don't skip."

Generally, Dr. Krym is a man of few words. *Don't* and *skip* are his favorites.

"I beg your pardon?" I asked.

I'd heard him.

"Don't skip."

I was buying a little time.

"I was thinking about how much money I owe you."

That's all.

No comment.

The first time I reached for a Kleenex, I pretended my back itched, and in scratching it against the business end of the couch, I moved my head to the left as if I had a crick in my neck and rolled my eyes upward and there he was, sitting at his desk with his back toward me and his elbow on the arm of the chair and his head in his hand, staring up at a little mirror—hanging as if from the ceiling of an airport bar—whose purpose I'd surmised was to clip nose hairs. All I could see was where his bald spot ended while he had me framed in extreme close-up.

"You do it with mirrors," I said. "Ha, ha."

Nothing.

I have a hunch if the two of us ever went for coffee we'd hit it off just fine.

"I saw Claire."

It's Phoebe's fault.

Her last paragraph to me before she retired to a little town up north called Paradise, which she deserves, was something to the effect that the mind is a dictator and the soul is a freedom fighter, which I promised her I'd think about. She also recommended Krym as a treasure not to be missed. And although I've been through the gauntlet at the clinic—I'd hoped to connect up with Dr. Gunther in the next office, who has my kind of legs and who practically forced me to identify all those vagina ink blots, or Dr. Feldman down the hall, who smiled in a fatherly fashion while he showed me those dreadful pictures—Krym picked me.

"With her little boy on the beach, I think she saw me. I'm almost positive she saw me sneak on her beach . . . with her little boy . . ."

Silence.

"I couldn't tell if it was a boy. I see her with a boy . . ."

". . . ."

"What are you writing? I can hear you writing."

"Just. Vun. Vord."

"I like your accent. I've never told you. I've always been partial to German." Not true.

"Cherman? You think my accent iss Cherman? I am from Vienna."

"Ah."

"You cannot tell Viennese from Cherman? Za difference iss vast."

"Sorry."

"Don't skip."

"She was fat."

"Claire vas fat? Zis iss inconsistent."

"Staci was fat. Is fat. Still."

"Ahhhhh." I heard his memory jog. "Arissona Staci."

"I'd never seen her in a bathing suit before."

"Arissona Staci?"

"Malibu Colony Claire."

I writhed a little.

"Don't skip."

"I was wondering if Mrs. Krym is fat, and I don't want to hurt your feelings again."

"No. Mrs. Krym iss not fat."

"She has enormous thighs."

"Repeat please?"

"With ripples all over them, and I massaged her and kneaded her flesh shoulder to toe, front to back, back to front . . ."

"Again?"

"Tuesday. And tried to force myself not to think about her husband . . . deputy sheriff six-four and mean . . . which helps . . ."

"Don't skip."

"Hey!"

"Vot?"

"Guess what?"

"Vot?"

"I'm not afraid to fly anymore!"

"Don't skip."

"A little maybe. She touches herself when she sees me on the tube . . . which helps . . ."

"Uf course."

"She looked private and was bent over like a mom, holding his hands and swinging his feet back and forth through the foam. I don't think she saw me. She has this astigmatism. I think I mentioned that, and when she's not wearing glasses she can barely see what's on her plate. You know what a crane looks like? You should've seen the bathing suit, he's a doctor . . ."

I TURNED RIGHT off Charleville onto Lasky Drive, squiggled across Wilshire, and right again on Santa Monica Boulevard. Two more rights and I'm going around in circles, I thought, which makes a wrong. To follow Charleville east through Beverly Hills back toward West Hollywood was certainly an option, a scenic option this time of year, but stop and go all the way—and lately I do things faster and notice less, I noticed. For no known reason I wound up in the wrong lane at La Cienega and missed my left.

Had a quick cup at Schwab's.

Nobody there.

Went home.

Took off my clothes down to my jockeys from Robinson's, made a muscle or two in the mirror, and filled out unemployment form 4581, rev. #30, on the john using *Variety* as a portable desk. I tripped over myself on the way from the bathroom to the bed and lay down for a nap.

That's when I got the phone call.

Mid-nap.

And you could have knocked me over with a whiff of Would You.

Did I remember her? That was her question to me. Did I possibly remember her?

Of course, I made it plain, I almost pleaded with her to accept the fact that I remember everything and hastily took the address in Inglewood.

Why not?

I am somewhat indefinitely in the mood for a Margie Cosgrove. Great gal, Margie. God. We had some times. We'll probably talk old times . . .

Don't skip.

She's a star fucker. I could hear it across the wires from far-off Inglewood.

On the other hand, I reminisce twice a week and pay through the nose for it.

I repeated the address on Arbor Vitae Street to be on the safe side, got off the phone as quickly as possible, the more to savor the near future. I looked around at my studio apartment on Holloway Drive and noticed almost no signs of the past, save a Georgia O'Keeffe print on the wall and an anthology of New York poets on the shelf, which were gifts. Then I took forever to wash the car.

THE LIGHTS went on at Ports.

Let's get the cows to Abilene.

"This is the cleanest goddamn car I ever saw."

"I had them spruce it up a little."

"You don't see that many Alfa Romeos in Fresno," she added, scootching my way, not easy in a Duetto Spyder.

Left on Santa Monica to La Brea, right on La Brea

(which doesn't make a right or a left or a right or a wrong onto Arbor Vitae because they're parallel). I think. In which case . . .

"I wondered whether your nose would be stuck up in the air," Margie continued thoughtfully. "Or something. When I called. I thought—you know—he's probably all mixed up in that Hollywood crowd . . ."

I nodded gravely.

"I thought you'd say, Margie Cosgrove . . . oh, well . . . that was way back then . . . you know . . ."

"No."

The freeway would have been the more direct route, but I don't know all the exits.

"Do you have to get up early tomorrow?" she asked the dashboard.

"No."

Left, I think on La Brea. No, on Florence. I'm already on La Brea. Or is it right? Do not pass airport. If you pass the airport you've gone too far.

"That's not the case," I said.

"Do you like my perfume?"

No. "Yeah."

"Sierra."

"No, I like it."

We drove for a spell in silence.

"God," she said.

"What?" I answered.

"I was just thinking . . ."

"About?"

Arbor Vitae is *perpendicular* to La Brea. One tends to think all is parallel in Inglewood.

"About how you used to play the piano at parties . . ."

"I used to play the piano?"

I never played the piano.

"At parties . . . and sing . . ."

I don't sing.

"Me?"

I hate parties.

"And do your imitations . . ."

"I did?"

"And do your imitations of Charley McCarthy and Mortimer Snerd."

I don't do the McCarthys. I do Barry Fitzgerald and Louis Armstrong.

"Ya-da-ya-da!"

"Huh?"

"Oye was just gettin' a wee moyt frus*trated* with *awl* these unfamiliar streets."

"It's the fourth house on the right. With the rose garden. Watch the curb."

I turned off the engine.

We sat.

For a while.

Each to our private side.

I became aware of the absence of drizzle on the windshield. "We don't have much drizzle in L.A. Remember the drizzle?"

Margie studied the windshield, recalling drizzle.

I would imagine.

Hard to tell in the dark.

"Do you want to come inside with me?"

"Yes." Which seemed like an ideal time to put my arm around her pink angora shoulders and recall Daisy Mae. I tilted her chin my way, à la Charles Boyer, and recognized chocolate candy eyes that I might have missed if the light had been better and the years not so wise. I kissed her candy and her cheeks and her chin, and second by second I conceded to time as I kissed her so gently all over the place. It surprised me, not so much the softness of her lips, but of mine, and I visualized myself out of the corner of an eye till a tiny adult jogged into my mind. "Not tonight."

We sat.

For a while.

Each to our private side.

And had a cigarette and succumbed to the whine of a low flying jet, for the airport is nearby.

"How many planes you seen take off?" Margie asked, being careful with her ashes. "And you know you shoulda been on 'em?"

Not enough. "All the time."

"Hah!" she said after a moment.

"What?"

"All I ever wanted to be was a princess on a goddamn spiral staircase."

"Hah!" I said.

"What?"

"All I ever wanted to be was an engaging prick."

"You?" she said. "Hah!"

Sometimes, I'm marvelously naive, I thought as we made our way through the rose garden and stood for a while by the door.

"Listen, write me, okay? And don't forget the picture. Do you ever get to Fresno? Hell, it's only two hours away. And we've got a pool 'n' stuff, and we could just lay around and tie one on. You'd like Harley—he's fulla jokes."

I resisted taking her key from her hand and opening the door. She knows about exits.

"Hey, remember those argyle socks I started to knit for you?"

I didn't. "I do."

"I never did finish the damn things. Hah! Is anybody crazier'n me?"

So I hugged her such a hug I nearly spilled the key. "Good night, my love."

And she looked at me as if I were a diving sunset. "Bye-bye, my hero."

I TOOK Arbor Vitae to Inglewood Avenue, hung a right, and recognized the young man of my dreams. *"You never told me you play the piano, kid."*

"She's crazy. You heard her. And where the hell have you been hiding?"

"Watch that tree!" Left on Manchester to the 405. *"Will you sing a song for me one day?"*

"I don't do parties, Lancaster."

"Can't wait to hear your Mortimer Snerd." North on 405 to the 10.

"Duh."

"Very nice, kid. Very nice." West on 10 to the public beach.

"Thank you."

"One thing I've always said about you, kid: underneath all that crap, you're too romantic for the real world." Plenty of parking places this time of the morning.

"Thank you."

He wanted to jog. At his age. He wanted to jog in damp grainy silence till one of us was spent.

Pretty spent.

So we sat on the beach for a while and caught our breath and pondered the flower lei and how it drifts . . .

. . . When in the middle of the best part he stood and strode to the water's edge and looked across and into the eye of the horizon and moved his great acrobat arm in an arc that cut a holy swath through the atmosphere, then whirled on me and seared my soul. *"Hear me, kid . . . I say we put a balcony on the car!"*

Burt smiled the incredible smile as we . . .

CUT TO:

Sunrise.

FADE IN:

THE END

ROLL CREDITS

Cast of contributors:

Joyce Brown.
Susan Shaw for so much.
Jonathan Mittleman for jazz.
Sasha Goodman, Joe Blades, Maryanne
Ziegler, L. Spencer Humphrey for uncommon
sense and inspiration.
Sharon Daley from the beginning.
Chronologically: Preston Jones, Bruce
Torrence, Git Polin, Aubrey Simms, Sondra
Farrell, Lev Mailer, Jo Corday, Robert Gist,
Maureen Foster, Patte Whitten, Gwynne
Gilford, Sharon Haberfeld, Robert Colbert,
Joey Walsh, Sidney Clute, Richard Jaeckel.
And throughout—my support group: Dan
Shor (The Mayor of New York), Jay Baker
(The Messiah), Roger Campo (Scout), and
the aforementioned Mittleman (The Bastard),
all of whom insist I suck ideas from them.

About the Author